Race to My Heart

Written by Aurora Parker

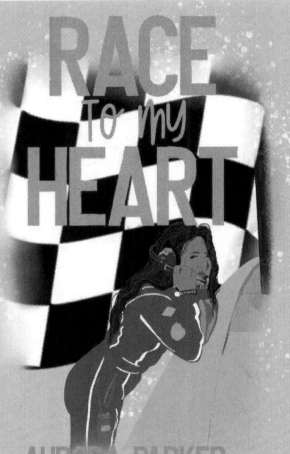

RACE
To my
HEART

AURORA PARKER

Table of Contents

Dougie

Grace

Dougie

Grace

Dougie

Grace

Dougie

Grace

Thank you for teaching me how to love the dirt.

I love you Poppa.

DRIFTWOOD BAY
POPULATION: 5000

CROISSANT CROSSING

THE WATERIN HOLE

4TH ST

5TH ST

FREEKY DEEKS

GULLY LN

6TH ST

PELICAN PL

STJRACING SHOP & TRACK

ST. JAMES POINT

Playlist

Bad Habits – Nerv

THE DEATH OF PEACE OF MIND - Bad Omens

Burn It Down – Parker McCollum

Over Now – Kameron Marlowe

Memory – Sugarcult

Twist Made Me – Lil Wayne

Lovers For The Weekend – John De Sohn

People Talk – Kidd G

Bite to Break Skin – Senses Fail

Coachella- Woodstock In Mind – Lana Del Ray

My Heart I Surrender – I Prevail

Love You Like That – Taylor Kade, KATT

Your Life and Mine – Just Surrender

If I Didn't Love You – Jason Aldean, Carrie Underwood

Better – Point North

Wilder Days – Morgan Wade

Heartbreak Anthem – Galantis, David Guetta, Little Mix

Wasn't That Drunk – Josh Abbott Band, Carley Pearce

Up To No Good – Warren Zeiders

Video Games – Lana Del Ray

This playlist can be found of Spotify by searching RTMH by Aurora Parker

Dougie

While slumped against the number fives fender, Dougie wiped the sweat beading across his forehead. The heat waves were already starting to come up across the horizon, threatening to sway reality. His eyes were glued to the dusty, two-mile oval dirt track that sat in front of him. He had a reddish-brown glow to his skin tone, which made it hard to tell if he was covered in dust from the track, forever stuck to his skin, or if his skin was forever pigmented from long hours spent in the hot summer sun, working on the car. Even on the most brutally hot days, if he could do his work outside, he would. His father always joked that he was cold blooded and needed the sun to warm him up. His dark skin emphasized prominent cheekbones and long limbs covered in tattoos. The dark, black ink snaked its way from his forearms all the way up to his neck. His hair falling to his shoulders, framing his warm, caramel brown eyes, despite the sweltering heat of the summers, he kept it long.

He had the thought and known deep within his bones that this was where his heart truly belonged. His entire life was focused on STJ Racing, starting from when he was just sixteen years old cleaning up after the mechanics, working his way up on Big Jims crew. Caring for and mastering every magnificent machine that ever adorned their track with great passion and sacrificing many of his younger years. However, it seemed that Dougie was never truly satisfied. Even after bringing his young brother Tanner on to drive, something from his life was still missing, and nearing thirty-three it was starting to gnaw into his every thought.

His undeniable contribution to shaping their renowned reputation gave him incredible leeway with the St. James family. Especially with their previous owner Jim, they had a mutual understanding that Dougie was here for the team, and he would do nothing to stop them from coming in number one.

Every.

Single.

Time.

And they succeeded year after year. Adding trophies to the seemingly never-ending wall.

Jim had been so pleased with Tanners driving, after Dougie brought him on. Everything Dougie asked for became a yes. Top of the line technology for optimized analytics? Yes. Brand new tires waiting on the racks? Not a problem. It made his life so much easier and honestly the crew was thriving. He had turned the team into a well-oiled machine, just like the cars they worked on. Everyone knew their purpose and place during the race. And Dougie was damn proud.

Dougie started to say in a slight melancholy tone, thinking of the blood, sweat and tears that lead them here, "T, I can't believe we are about to start another season." Tanner as usual was glued to his brother's side. Everything around the track turned into a two-man job the duo would no doubtable handle.

Tanner scoffed jokingly "Another trophy will be up on the shelf soon enough" his smirk widening as he took in the surrounding view of the track. The dark, dusty soil contradicting the light sandy beaches and forever blue skies that spread out just beyond the end of the track.

"Do you remember all the time we used to spend with dad in the garage? I felt like he would keep us locked in there for hours every single weekend." Dougie and Tanner would spend endless hours by their father's side, obediently passing him any tool he asked for, cherishing the opportunity to help him.

Tanner's blue eyes sparkled as his lips stretched into a smile,

"Yeah, and you wouldn't know how to build an engine if dad had me holding the flashlight for him, instead of you. You watched and he talked to you about it. I mostly sat in the front seat and tried not to die of boredom, he never let me do anything besides let me get him a beer." Tanner was five years younger than Dougie.

Dougie rolled his eyes at the thought of little Tanner getting his dad a beer from the fridge. But the kid was probably right and got the old man a beer or two every so often. His hands being too small to hold the bottles. Their dad wasn't the best father, he tried his hardest to be a single dad of two boys after their mother ran out on them, looking for a bigger life than the small town had to offer. But working on cars was their dad's escape… it brought him back to life, and if it was something he could do with his boys, they were going to enjoy it too.

Dougie shook his head sadly, the corners of his mouth twitching in a smile. "I was getting yelled at for doing it wrong and you were getting left alone, that sounds way better. Plus, I'm pretty sure you used to play 'race car'," Dougie couldn't help but hold out his arms in front of him like he was gripping a stirring wheel and made screeching noises as if his imaginary car was speeding along the curves of track. Thank god it was just the two of them out here.

"Oh yeah!" Tanner chuckled, "I guess he really had us set in our ways, even back then." Both men erupted into full belly laughs. Tanner's laugh was like his brothers but lighter, Dougie's laugh was deep and dark.

Douggie's involvement amongst the crew was much more extensive than simply providing car maintenance. He was the heart and soul of the team, constantly aware of what was going on with the cars and actively participating in every aspect of racing. STJ Racking had three cars that they rotated through depending on how reckless the drivers could be during the season. Last year they did well, only needing to replace a few outer parts here and there but no major wrecks. Tanner was still a young driver and let his ego get the best of his emotions a time or two, but what we've all been there before. It's just a little different when he's sitting behind the wheel of a multi hundred-thousand-dollar machine that could kill him with one wrong turn.

Tanner gave his brother a tender pat on the back, tightening his grip, "You've been my constant support. In the racing world and elsewhere, throughout the never-ending loops. There's no one I would want by my side on this crazy earth."

Blinking back the water that started to form in his eyes was nearly impossible. They came from a family that never publicly displayed love, and this broke their hearts. However, as they entered adulthood, the guys vowed solemnly to end the pattern of emotional distance. It had been a hard road, but they made great strides to be more open with each other about the things in their lives that were important. Nothing was more important to Dougie than family. All he had was Tanner now that their father had passed away and their mother was MIA. She never showed up for the funeral and the guys had tried reaching out to hear with unanswered text messages and full voicemail boxes.

The Williams brothers' relationship ran deep, their relationship was forged not only by shared ties to family, but also by their shared desire for triumph on the racetrack. Any parent can force an activity on their child and hope to god they love it. For Mr. Williams, he struck gold with his sons. They took to cars like flies on honey.

Tanner had been protected by Dougie for his entire life, saving him from any obstacles that might stand in the way of his success, both on and off the racetrack. His younger sibling had an odd talent for always finding a spark of mischief wherever he went, which always resulted in mayhem. But big brother was always there to fix everything that had gone wrong and had a way to clean up the mess.

Every late-night text, every phone call, Dougie was there to support his brother, it was more than what their mother had done. Being five years older, he took the responsibility of big brother seriously. Sometimes he swore his mother noticed Dougie being a better parent than she could be and took that to justify leaving. She saw that he picked up all the pieces she had dropped and left behind.

The faint sound of approaching footsteps suddenly snapped the brothers' out of wandering focus, no one needed to see them all emotion in front of the track, the crew would never let them hear the end of it. Those guys could be brutal.

In the stillness of the afternoon, the piercing sound of heels striking concrete echoed throughout the lot, like shots across a battlefield. They turned toward the sound of the noise only to see Grace St. James striding towards them. Her long black hair framing her petite silhouette in the summer sun, the yellow sundress accentuating her tan skin, gently billowing in the breeze around her. She was the team's new 'managing owner'; as her father had called it, during the meeting at the end of last season announcing his retirement and her takeover. They had known for some time that Jim was planning on retiring, but everyone had assumed Grace's brother, Damon, would take his place.

Dougie watched her approach and his brows furrowed in sadness and rage. As Grace took charge of the team, he felt a twinge of regret for not talking to Jim. But he also realized it would have never been him to take over the team, sure he was there as a paid hand, but never to run. It was hard to overlook why it had to be her, this was her family legacy... not that she had spent much time around it in the past five years. She had ditched the dirt to go after pavement as soon as she turned eighteen. Yes, he could admit that she did have the experience from growing up around the track, but dirt was a whole different ball game compared to the pricks over on the pretty blacktop.

Being a woman in the racing world was tough. That's why there weren't that many of them, he could only count five with ease off the top of his head. The Old Timers generously contributed a sizable sum of money through sponsorships to our team, her team, providing us with significant financial support. But that also came with their old-world view on racing and where women should be, we'll give you a hint...at home. Many of these guys couldn't take women in racing seriously and often tried to discount their success.

While Dougie didn't necessarily think racing should revert to the ways of colonists, he did think Grace was a stuck up, spoiled, overindulged princess. She drives a blacked out BMW for Christ sake. Sticking out like a sore thumb in their dusty beach town filled with cruisers and wranglers.

Does she really think she can come in here with a swoop and run the place? He couldn't help but think. This tiny woman standing in front of him did not have the heart or the guts to take them all the way to the top. He gave her three weeks. Tops.

One bad season and those sponsorships would be gone. The St. James' family trust could only bail the team out for so long before the well ran dry. Racing was not a cheap sport, four tires could cost anywhere from ten to fifteen thousand dollars, not to mention the cost of fuel for the race or god forbid needed a brand-new engine. His heart was filled with a deep rage that grew more intense with each passing second, thinking about what he and Tanner would do next if this team no longer existed. If the team crumbled, then the track would surely close after that then the town of Driftwood Bay would be no more. It surely wouldn't be able to attract the level of tourists it needed to sustain itself on its own. Driftwood Bay needed the track just as much as the track needed Driftwood Bay.

"Morning guys!" she waved, "How's it going?" she was trying to mask that he was making her nervous, her voice wavering slightly, Her eyes unable to stay on his for more than a few seconds. He read right through that mask. Dougie managed a feeble nod while desperately trying to maintain his composure, his eyes brimming with rage. He didn't know what would come out of his mouth if he dared to speak.

"Yes, we've spent the past week, and entire offseason getting ready." Tanner grumbled. Clearly annoyed with her asking such an obvious question as if she hadn't been watching them all off season from her office window.

Though unintentionally sarcastic, Dougie's mouth burst open "What do you think this is? Amateur hour?" he basically spat, bitterness shining through every word. He could feel Tanner staring at him, trying to bore a hole through to his brain to see what hell he was thinking. He didn't know why she had come over to try and make conversation with them, she would have been better off just parking her car in the surface lot next to the track and waving as she walked inside. She needed to learn her place to stay in the office and leave them to winning.

He didn't even know what fuck he was thinking. He never spoke out of turn like that, especially with ownership. Normally he only spoke like that in private with Tanner.

Grace looked at Dougie, a glint of curiosity shimmering in the depths of her emerald eyes. "To say that I would ever doubt your abilities, Dougie, is disheartening. You are without a doubt a key partner on this team." Her voice matched the same sarcastic tone as his. Fine, she wanted to play checkers, well let's give her the best fucking game of chess she's ever played.

Dougie sighed, his words tinged with sarcasm, a smidgen of resentment, and a hint of sorrow. "Maybe, but I don't think daddy's little princess truly understands the enormous passion and dedication we put into this sport," He said leaning in a little closer to where she stood. Being sure to look down on her. He was by no means a monster of a man, but her petite frame made his six-foot two tower over hers.

He looked at Tanner in the hopes that he would give him some assurance, maybe even some back up, but Tanner was staring off into the distance, seemingly longing to run away and jump into the ocean to avoid listening to his brother dig a hole he wouldn't be able to climb out of.

Grace's lips curled into a bitter smile "Dougie, I long to reveal the truth to you," dramatically bringing her hand to her chest. "Oh, is that how you see it? You are the see-er of paths and journeys? Believe it or not, despite coming from a castle, it has been a difficult journey for me to get here." She looked him up and down, all playfulness draining from her eyes. She was laying the drama on thick and it was annoying the shit out of him.

"You can call me Princess once you start to respect me." She snapped. "But until then, its Ms. St. James to you."

Dougie's eyebrow shot up his forehead but before he could speak Grace turned on her heel and marched off to fulfill her the rest of whatever it is her obligations were , not letting him get in the last word.

What the actual fuck just happened? He thought to himself and why the fuck did T leave him out high and dry. So much for always having each other's backs.

A mixture of caution and curiosity swirled in the depths of Dougie's eyes as he fixed his gaze on her round ass against his better judgment, prolonging the moment longer than he had intended, as she walked away from them. He was unable to ignore the intense flame, her unwavering determination, or those emerald pools she had for eyes.

With a playful poke of his elbow and a twinkle of mischief in his eyes, Tanner gently prodded Dougie.

"I think you met your match this season, she's going to give you a run for your money."

A moment of amusement, Dougie's small laugh served

to lessen the severity of the shadows in his face.

"We will see, brother. We will see."

Grace

The coastal town of Driftwood Bay was bathed
in the vibrant glow of the sun's rays, infusing the sandy
coastline with a vibrant energy and enchanting
brilliance. The exact opposite of how Grace was feeling
after her run in with Dougie and Tanner out by the track.
This season was going to be harder than she originally
thought, not that she was expecting this to be easy. But
she wasn't expecting Tanner and Dougie to be complete

jerks to her. Well Dougie was mostly the ass, and Tanner just stood there in La La land.

Located in the serene northern region of North Carolina, this enchanting seaside town proudly showcased a picturesque collection of delightful pastel residences, dating back to colonial times, majestic sand dunes that stood tall, and draped in whimsical beach grass that danced joyfully with the wind. Truly captivating all who witnessed it. The townspeople were just as magical as the mirage the coastline created. Weaving through the vibrant main streets, one can encounter a treasure trove of charming family-owned shops and restaurants, each contributing its own unique charm to the lively atmosphere.

The summer season brought a bountiful spell of tourists to the town, as every business thrived and reaped abundant rewards following the triumphant victories from STJ Racing… except we lost. Race One, week one, a big fat L next to Tanner Williams name on this seasons roster, and the STJ Racing logo. The first race had been an absolute disaster. Grace had stayed in the pits with the rest of the crew instead of going up to the owner's box. She wanted to be back in the mess of it all. It ended up being a complete mess for sure.

Watching Tanner drive had been like watching a preschooler try to climb up a steep playground slide. Move forward a few inches, then slide back down a few feet. It was downright frustrating to watch, and she was doing everything to keep from screams like a grown man at the TV. She kept her spirits high around the crew though, cheering encouraging words that caused some strange sideways glances to be tossed her way. She was just trying to not be a Debbie downer, yet she wanted to drown her sorrows in mint chip ice cream.

*   *   *   *   *   *   *   *

The team was eagerly gearing up for another invigorating day at the track when she pulled into her parking spot. She made a mental note to have the stupid 'owners parking' sign removed later today. It's not like they had to fight each other for parking.

Grace had emailed Dougie and Tanner late Sunday night asking if any improvements could be made to the car or their strategy but received no response back, which didn't surprise her. When she pulled up to the track that morning she could see Dougie walking towards the shop, hopefully he had some insight into what the hell went on this weekend. She took deep, calming breaths to help keep her Zen attitude. She had meditated that more and refused to let an ounce of negative energy sway her mindset. It was just one race but setting a precedent like that amongst the other teams right out the gate, was not a good look. She was going to do everything she could to keep her family's legacy afloat. Not that they were drowning, that would insinuate this losing thing would become a regular occurrence. Which was not the St. James way.

From her car she could also see Tanner, radiating an irresistible charm that only the star racer possesses. His captivating ocean blue eyes and radiant golden locks effortlessly attained the attention of onlookers, who couldn't help but be mesmerized. With an air of nonchalance, he leaned against a flawlessly crafted race car, which Dougie most likely meticulously inspected, like he did every morning.

Even with all the windows up in her car, she was still able to hear the roar that came from the direction of the shop.

"Don't lean on the fucking car, how many times do I have to tell you that?"

Damn, Dougie really was meticulous about the car and that roar was downright ferocious. She couldn't help but laugh to herself hoping her email had gotten under their skin, she didn't mind causing them a little extra tension this morning.

Grace emerged from the car; her delicate figure further enhanced by another breezy summer dress gathered at her waist, accentuating her subtly yet alluring curves. It was too hot to wear anything skintight, the sweltering heat already causing sweat to form on the small of her back.

Her magnificent, luscious black hair cascaded down her back, capturing the radiant sunbeams reminiscent of a velvet waterfall. Confidence in every step, and determination shining bright in her eyes, she approached Dougie and Tanner, who exchanged a subtle glance that spoke volumes. She had known Dougie was somehow behind the loss, there was absolutely no reason for Tanner to suddenly forget what it took to win. She looked at the two of them standing there, smug smiles on their faces. Something was up and she was going to find out.

"I know you boys are up to something," Grace declared, her voice beaming, with extra emphasis on the word boys, as if to point out that they are acting like children. Because they were. "I just don't know what yet." She pointed a finger between the two of them. She had to admit they were intimidating, standing next to each other. One taller and larger than the other.

Dougie squinted his eyes ever so slightly, thoroughly assessing Grace, as doubt danced beneath his composed demeanor, steadily intensifying like a gentle flame. Through his perspective, she truly exemplified everything he truly detested about the world of racing - a privileged young women with a silver platter. One who failed to understand the relentless dedication and immense sacrifices required to achieve victory, forever using her family's last name like a credit card. However, she was anything, ANYTHING, but a princess and she was going to prove it to them.

"Do you even have the tenacity to lead this team? Do you truly comprehend the sheer dedication, perseverance, and sacrifice required in the world of racing?" Dougie's words resonated with fervor that pierced the air. He wasn't giving her an inch, not even a little bit. But this wasn't the first time he had questioned her dedication to the team. He had no clue what her journey had been like when she left Driftwood Bay at eighteen. Nascar was a whole different ball game that she had learned to play, and an even bigger boys club than the two men in front of her were trying to instill. She was ready to take that smug smile and shove it back where it had come from. Grace responded to his skepticism with an unwavering stare, her eyes ablaze with resolve.

"Although I may not have spent my childhood with grease up to my elbows, Douglass. Do not underestimate my burning zeal for racing. I'm here to not only demonstrate my worth to you, but to each and every member of this remarkable team." She winked.

With a swift motion, she circled her slender finger above her head, mimicking a lasso, symbolizing her limitless determination. "Do you grasp the significance of that?" She exclaimed assertively, nose wrinkling like she smelled a stench that would not clear, perturbed by his words. She extended another slender finger towards him and took a step closer so she could stand on her tip toes, to whisper in his ear.

"Always remember to choose your words wisely, I sign your fucking paycheck." If he was going to play the 'you don't know shit, little girl' nonsense she just escaped, she would play right back. It takes two to tango and she was here to fucking dance.

Tanner, always the mischievous yet insightful individual, cheekily interrupted with a radiant smile. "Don't you remember how stubborn she is bro?"

Tanner and Grace had been friends for years, constantly at the track together when they were younger, but it was always hard to tell who Tanner was rooting for more, Grace or Dougie. Even with spending so much time with one brother, the other was a complete enigma to her. Dougie's eyes danced between Grace and Tanner, entangled in a mesmerizing inner battle.

With unmatched speed, she swiftly turned on her heel and departed. Lost in her own thoughts hoping to run to the safety of her office. Sitting on the second level of the shop and windows that overlooked the parking lot, delivery bays, and track- she had a full view of her domain, which also made a great hiding spot. The office was her fathers and grandfathers long before her renovations gave it a fresh face with light beiges and blues to bring the comfort of the beach inside.

* * * * * * * *

Dougie found himself embracing a captivating blend of curiosity and defiance. He understood this season was bound to be extraordinary. Grace's mere presence electrified the team, infusing it with a vibrant energy that was starting to captivate him despite his initial doubts.

* * * * * * * *

In the days that ensued, Grace found immense joy in immersing herself in the daily intricacies of the crew, embracing every chance to expand her knowledge and she flourished. The crew was abuzz with curiosity and happiness, not used to experiencing such a hands-on owner. Her father had been a hands-on guy but he didn't sit in the shop with the mechanics asking questions.

Dougie was hating every second of it and she was eating it the fuck up. She could count a multitude of times she caught him scowling in her direction whenever she was working with Tanner or one of the other guys.

When she wasn't working in the trenches with the crew, Grace had herself locked up in her office watching over hours of competitor footage. She needed a leg up this season, if Tanner and Dougie weren't going to hand her the win like they would her father, she would have to take it for herself. Even though she knew that Tanner's loss was nothing but 'human error' as Dougie called it, she still craved to know every detail of the other teams she was up against. There was no way this entire season would end in a loss.

*   *   *   *   *   *   *   *

Knowing she was up there; Dougie couldn't help himself from glancing up at the windows every so often. Through the big glass rectangles, he could see her nestled up in the cozy corner of the L shaped couch that sat facing the track. On clear days, that was a great spot to watch the race if you didn't want to get dirty. Big Jim used to say it was the "Ladies Room" on race day. All the wives would congregate in the office, drinking, while the men sat in the boxes above the grandstands.

As if just by thinking about her, something caused her to stir from the couch. Quickly before her eyes could meet his, Dougie crept back into the shadows of the garage.

Dougie

As the dawn broke over the slumbering town, rage boiled beneath Dougie's skin, and if he wasn't careful, he was going to lose control. He hadn't slept a wink last night. He had thought he had his anxiety handled but thoughts of losing overwhelmed his brain for the entirety of the night. Tossing and turning through the early hours. Another loss this week and we would look like chumps.

Rolling out of bed, no longer able to sleep, he showered, changed, and got ready for the day. Every part of his morning routine was meticulous, each step pushing and soothing the anxiety away. At a young age Dougie learned to throw himself into his projects to help his mind stay in the present moment instead of wandering to the what ifs.

He pulled on his usual black shortsleeved, button up shirt with the STJ logo embroidered on the left chest and a boot cut pair of black jeans, there was no bother to wear anything else. He always ended up covered in dust or grease anyways. He also loved not having to pull an outfit together, he laughed to himself thinking about having to wear a suit to an office every day.

Turning left off his block onto main street, he quickly maneuvered into a spot in front of Freaky Deeks at the last second. Suddenly coffee sounded like exactly what he needed. It was our well-known coffee spot owned and operated by none other than Deacon 'Freaky Deeks' Benton. He made a great cup of coffee and for the most part left Dougie the fuck alone, unlike the other gossips that filled the town with senseless noise.

"Do you happen to know what Grace St. James orders?" he asked the young girl behind the counter. Surprising himself at how this plan was turning out, he needed to have a chat with her, and coffee seemed like the friendly way to go. The girl behind the counter had to be no more than seventeen, pretty in a spends the summers in the sun freckles splattering her nose, type of way. This was a small town with only one coffee shop, the girl had to know. A voice came from behind him before the cashier had a chance to speak.

"She gets an iced latte, with skim milk and one pump of caramel," turning around, behind him stood

Baillie Post, Grace's best friend. Similar in height to Grace, Baillie stood at a peitite five foot two but despite her lack of heigh she was furiously passionate about anything at any given time. The fire that raged in her soul fed the passion that poured out of her. Her blonde hair was up in a tight ponytail, and she looked like she just got back from a run. Great. The whole town was going to find out he was buying Grace coffee.

"Getting the new boss, a cup of coffee," she chirped as she smiled at the teenager who walked off to make his order. He refused to play into her game, letting the awkward silence linger instead. It was none of Baillie's business what he was up to.

Handing the cashier a twenty when she finally came back with his two drinks, he quickly grabbed them off the counter, mumbling a goodbye to Baillie, as if a cat had got his tongue, and dashed out the door before Baillie could say anything else. Since when couldn't he talk to women in this town?

The scorching, summer heat unleashed its tantalizing secret, whispering promises of untold wealth to the town. Every business stood at the ready, eager to taste the sweet fruits of success once STJ Racing started winning. The anticipation thick in the air and the line wrapping around Freaky Deeks was no joke- there had to be at least 10 people in line already as Dougie barged out the front doors.

Tourist flocked into town the week of the race usually staying Wednesday through Wednesday, that's what most of the rentals allowed, so they could get the full beach and racing weekend experience. It was a win-win for rents, business owners and locals alike. No matter what was going on in Driftwood Bay, everyone in town could be found at the track on Saturday Nights.

Bright stadium lights illuminating through the darkness with thick clouds of smoke billowing into the sky. People lived for it, many families returning summer after summer.

He knew that Saturday had to be nothing short of extraordinary, the next thrilling chapter in their racing journey. He was the first one to the shop almost every morning and today was no different. Instead of waiting in the shop for the rest of the crew to mosey their way in, making morning small talk he usually loved. He headed for the stairs and climbed up to the offices, both coffees in hand.

The distant growl of an engine pierced through the silence, Grace must have just pulled in. Should he make himself comfy on her couch and surprise her or should he wait outside like a lion stalking his prey. He ran his hand over his face, unsure of what to do, suddenly settling on leaving the coffee on her desk for her to discover. Possibly never knowing it was him. The sharp click clack of shoes down the hallway popped his thought bubble, he was completely trapped in her office. There was only one hallway that led to the stairs and her office was at the very end. There was no way he wouldn't run into her. Well, no backing out now.

"Is that for me?" she smirked, pointing a long finger in the direction of the iced latte in his hand.

His smile never faltered "Let me guess, Baillie called you?"

"Oh no" she looked surprised and tilted her head like a golden retriever confused at its owner's command. Well with that long black hair, it would be more of a black lab. At the mention of Baillie's name Grace chuckled and smiled "but now I'll call her after you leave. But you do have two coffees in your hands, and one suspiciously looks like my order." Taking a long swig from the iced coffee he handed her, she thanked him and started setting up her desk for the day.

"I was hoping we could chat for a bit about the week ahead of us?" he questioned, sitting down on the couch.

* * * * * * * *

"Last week's loss was a fucking fluke," He bellowed, "how many times do I need to say that before you get that through your thick skull, woman?" They had been sitting in her office for over an hour going back and forth over the data from last week's race. Grace was becoming increasingly suborn finding it hard to believe that Tanner suddenly forgot how to drive. Like he had lost all his spark behind the wheel.

A screech so loud, he thought the windows were going to break came out of her mouth followed by a high pitch "Not on opening weekend!!!" He was pretty sure the whole bay just heard what came from her mouth.

Damn, that chicks got a set of pipes. She was right, they shouldn't have lost that race and he had to get down to the bottom of what the fuck was going on with Tanner. But she was out of her mind to get this worked up.

Ushering him out her door, as she would hear no more. He made his way down to the shop to cool off from the battle upstairs. She was so fucking arrogant. Shit happens and she needs to let it go, this week would be different. All he wanted to do was talk about strategy for the season and she had all these grandiose plans from the footage she had been watching. None of that was going to help them. Tanner needed to stay true to his driving style and they would preserver as always. She needed to let the men do their work.

"What did you do this time?" Tanner laughed from where he was sitting on the other side of the shop bay. So much for finding solitude and calming down.

Maybe a walk around the track would have been a better idea. Tanner was bound to annoy him with some stupid question that he didn't have time for today.

"I told her last week was a fluke and you're an incredible driver. We aren't changing a damn thing about the way we race. If it continues to happen then we will reassess but as of right now, it's not necessary." he started pacing around the workbenches, "There is nothing we need to change, one race doesn't mean we throw everything out and start from the ground up again," Tanner agreed and shook his head back and forth. Oh, he wasn't expecting Tanner's complete support. He really thought the kid had a soft spot for Grace, but this was music to his ears.

"I understand the shriek now. Don't worry dude, if she's telling me to do one thing, I'm doing the opposite. I know how to win, and I know how to race. Those other guys just out strategized me. But I've been workin' on it all week."

"Yea she can sing for sure." Was all Dougie said. Letting his brother's words fully sink in.

The rest of the week continued without incident, he could thank god. Grace had done a steady job of staying in her office and Dougie had held up his end, motivating and encouraging the team, despite the pressures that lay ahead. Tanner kept to his word of working on strategy and he spent countless hours out on the track.

* * * * * * * *

Grace locked eyes with Dougie and Tanner early Saturday morning as they were getting prepped for the day ahead, bracing herself for the impending challenge. Cornering them in the shop bay before they were able to escape to the track. Both men let out a heavy sigh as she made her way over to where they were standing.

" We must win or at least place in the top three minimum. MINIMUM. Nothing else is an option. There is a lot of pressure here and we need to show off. It's a sold out crowd tonight" the brothers looked between themselves, realizing it wasn't going to be the last time someone else's livelihood depended on their performance. Dougie glanced towards the grandstands and parking lot that was already starting to fill up with the other teams.

"Do you grasp that?" She retorted fiercely, clearly agitated by their lack of answer. Her slender finger extended, waving it between their heads. She was on a roll today.

"Why are you both so quiet?" she asked, a sinister glint in her eyes.

"Do you think this is the first time we've been

given this little speech before," Dougie said as he looked

her up and down, sarcasm dripping off each word, but

his eyes lingered on the curve of her breasts a little too

long. He couldn't help but wonder what her skin felt like

through her sheer top.

With a sly smile, Tanner couldn't resist but

interrupt. "Don't worry Gracie-girl, we got this on lock

and in the bag," He gestured in the air like he was

grabbing something off the top shelf and shoving it in a

make-believe bag.

Despite their long-standing friendship, Tanner

noticed a chilling glaze in Grace's gaze towards Dougie.

Looking directly at Dougie as she spoke "I have as much

faith in you, as I do in that bag of air your brother is

holding," jerking her thumb in the direction of Tanner's

air bag. He couldn't help but smirk. He loved how fired

up she was getting; he had never had a woman come

back at him with such fire in her eyes. He loved a bit of banter.

Dougie's eyes darted back and forth, torn between Grace and Tanner, entangled in a tormenting battle within himself. "Are you saying you don't have faith in Tanner's ability to win?" he questioned, mocking her. Easily throwing the conversation back to Tanner. He wanted her gaze off of him immediately, it was making him sweat.

"No nimrod," she jabbed a painted nail into his chest "I have zero faith in you," With an abruptness that matched her arrival, she walked away.

"Good going meathead, way to piss her off this early in the day. Now she's going to be pissy for the next twelve hours and we'll be stuck with her in our ears." Tanner shook his head and wandered off to finish getting his head ready for the race.

Dougie couldn't shake the intense swirl of

animosity and fascination that engulfed him. He couldn't help but replay the words repeatedly in his head *'I have no faith in you'* which is what he had been told his entire life, just but someone who should have loved him and had faith in him unconditionally. The only person who ever had any faith in him was Tanner and watching him walk away the way he just did was tearing Dougie's insides apart. Whatever was going on between him and Grace needed to be kept far away from Tanner.

* * * * * * * *

The last hour before the start of the race was always the worst, the checklist of everything Dougie could have forgotten starts rolling like a ball down a steep hill that won't stop until it hits the very bottom. A competitor could be disqualified, which would screw up the starting positions, the engine could magically fail inspection for whatever god knows reason, the list went on and on. Dougie fought to keep the clarity in his vision, the corners starting to blur as his anxiety crept up his spine. He shook his head to try and shake the feeling.

Finally, the drivers are called to their vehicles, his eyes scan the crowd for Grace, hoping to catch a glimpse of her in the owner's box. Last race she had surprised the team by staying in the pits with them for the entire race. Normally the owners would stay in the boxes, where they would have a better, more expansive view of the race. The boxes also had large TVs, alcohol, and food. But to his surprise, he turned around to find her chatting with one of the tire guys, Vinny. He hoped she was going to head up to the box once the race started, he didn't need her down here distracting anyone from the race. Hell, he could have blamed her last week's loss. The team wasn't used to having the boss in the pits with them.

A voice came through the speakers announcing

the race would be starting momentarily. The sounds of engines starting and revving filled the air. A gentle hum buzzed in his check. Dougie grabbed his headphones and stalked over to his usual spot amongst the team, right in front, dead center.

"Check," he spoke into the mouthpiece connected to his headphones, "you read me T?"

"Yeah, loud and clear, good to go," Tanner came through on the other end. They would be connected during the entire race through the Bluetooth headphone set in Tanners helmet and in Dougie's red ear covers.

Engines roared as the stands came to life celebrating the start of the race. Pulling off the track, the pace car went past the teams as the green flag was put out, waving in the wind signaling the cars to start whipping around the track. The dust already turning the blue sky a dirty brown. Off in the corner something caught his eye, taking his eyes off the race for a moment, he found Grace standing amongst the team against the railing, with her own set of headphones on.

"No box today?" he called out to her, forgetting his microphone was still live.

"What," both Grace and Tanner said simultaneously.

"Fuck sorry T not you," but before his brother could answer, instead of going left with the curve of the track, Tanner's car slammed into the wall on his right.

Grace

Thoughts of another loss consumed Grace as she walked down main street, headed to the track. Her mind was lost in all the ways she's failed in her role so far. She was sure letting her family down and couldn't imagine what her grandfather was thinking. She had avoided his call yesterday and had seriously been putting off calling him back. Maybe on her walk home she would stop by their house to say hi, using her memaw as a buffer.

In the early morning hours, unable to sleep, she had emailed the entire crew calling for yet another team meeting. She hoped they wouldn't show up with pitchforks. She had absolutely no idea what she was going to say, everything she tried to rehearse in her head sounded moronic and robotic. There was no reason for what happened on Saturday other than Dougie being completely distracted, nothing was adding up and she was starting to feel like they were out to get her. She crossed her fingers that they wouldn't show up with pitchforks just in case.

She was also going to need a very large cup of coffee from Deeks. Coffee was just about the only thing making her happy at this point besides her three pm Diet Coke with lime.

Comfort always trumped style for Grace and

there was no way she would ruin her good shoes walking a mile to work in them. Hoka sneakers were her go too and she swore they made her walk faster.

Even though it was just dirt racing, she liked to look good. "Looking good means, you feel good," her mother always would say. However, Grace chose not to wear too much makeup and focused on skincare, letting the sun highlight her skin naturally, using just enough brown mascara to enhance her naturally dark eyelashes and brows which matched her long, black hair. She was also keen on making sure her hair stayed shiny and curled- she absolutely loved her hair. It was her most favorite asset. She had a memory from kindergarten of wanting to cut her hair short like one of her friends and spent the entire weekend crying to her memaw, missing her long hair.

After finishing college at Duke, Grace had

realized she wanted to stay in Driftwood Bay for good. Even though her siblings and parents had left a long time ago to live further inland, she still craved the salty ocean air. Her grandparents also lived locally, which was also a major plus. She and her memaw were incredibly close, speaking on the phone almost every day and Pops was too old to come to the races now with his breathing problems, but he still watched every Saturday on the local sports channel. She was honestly surprised they still broadcasted local sports on cable, she knew the race was streamable but she didn't have much faith in herself to teach her grandfather how to set it up. The cable worked great for his needs, and she loved him for it.

She purchased a small beach bungalow, with her grandparents help, about a mile off the main strip, just close enough to town and the track for a brisk morning walk, but far enough away that she had a pair of heels in her bag to swap with her sneakers when she got to her office. She was also one street over from her grandparents' house. She knew her parents found solace in knowing someone from the family still lived close to them.

The other thing she loved about her bungalow was that it wasn't just called a beach bungalow for its light, airy decor, but for the fact that the ocean was just steps from her front door. The beach was the only place lately that Grace felt like she could take a deep breath and fully expand her lungs. Every night for the past few weeks she's loved sitting out on her back patio practicing her breathing and listening to the calming sounds of the waves. It was working wonders for her anxiety. She managed to stop picking at her cuticles, which was a nasty habit she had been trying to quit for some time.

But by the time she finally strolled into the shop

garage bays, after stopping at Deeks and wandering slowly to the shop, she only had a few minutes before her meeting call time. Which she was deeply regretting sending. The glares sent around the room were basically the same as pitchforks. Actually, she would have preferred a physical pitchfork than the death stares. She should have gotten coffee for everyone, she though looking down at the latte in her hand.

She said her hellos and good mornings, making her way around the group to make her way to the front of the room, trying to ease some of the tension. She found a small step stool so she could see everyone. Hopefully she didn't look like a pompous asshole, but clearly too late for that!

"Alright, Good Morning everyone!" she started clapping her hands together. yep– total asshole.

"Thank you for coming in early, I really appreciate it- I know my email was a little last minute!"

She chuckled and paused hoping the rest of the group would laugh a little.

Nope.

Crickets.

"I just wanted to touch base with everyone and let you know that one set back is not going to put any doubt in my mind about what this team is capable of accomplishing." she paused for effect again, crossing her fingers that it was working. She hoped her enthusiasm would leech onto the crew, "This team hasn't had three losses in a row since '06 and if this week shit hits the fan, that's 0-3 for STJRacing. This team is a family, win or lose. So, let's pull up our bootstraps and get this car into first place!" Looking around the room, a few people gave a small woot…it wasn't much but she would take all the support she could get. "Alright, alright I know everyone is still asleep," she mellowed her enthusiasm only slightly, waving her hands forward as if to shoo them from the room "Let's get the day started."

Everyone started to disperse, stopping at the coffee machines first. Grace wandered over to the wall where they shelved all the trophies, every year was represented by a three foot tall, gold shining cup with a car on the top. The only year missing was '06. Even after her grandfather had replaced the driver that lost three races in a row, the team could never recover that year. Maybe they placed 5th or 6th but she couldn't remember clearly. All she was clear on was that they didn't win.

Ironically right across from the trophy wall, as the team dubbed it, sat the wrecked car from last week, taunting her. She was asking for a lot of the team this week. After Tanner's crash last week, they had a lot of work to do. There wasn't major frame damage, but he tore up the thirty-thousand-dollar paint job real good, and plenty of metal work that needed to be done to keep the car in one piece. She was close to telling them to switch out the car with one of the others they had, but she hesitated. Her gut had a feeling that this losing streak wasn't ending any time soon and she would rather keep wrecking the same car than majorly damage all three.

Looking down at her watch, Grace realized she had spent far too much time wandering about the shop reminiscing on racing past. Briskly walking up to her office, Grace pulled out her phone and dialed her best friend.

"I think I scared them into submission," she joked to her best friend Baillie, when she finally picked up the phone on basically the last ring. What else could that girl be doing besides pick up her calls.

"This early? It's not even 10 am yet?" her best friend laughed through the other end of the phone.

Baillie knew how intense Grace could be at any hour.

"I mentioned '06" Grace answered roughly, knowing how silly that sounded to anyone unfamiliar with their history.

"Oh, shit you did?" Baillie laughed, "You could scare any race fan, let alone grown men, with that story. Do they know the driver was your uncle?" Grace forgot that Baillie knew the true story of 06. That the driver had been her uncle Beau. That season caused a massive rift in the family. Beau still hasn't spoken to his father since and moved west shortly after the blow out. Clearly the St. James's were stubborn and good at holding grudges.

"Probably the older guys that have been with us, or if anyone asked why there wasn't an '06 trophy, but I don't think anyone openly talks about it." she shrugged as if Baillie could see her through the phone.

"Need drinks later to cheer you up? We could go to The Watering Hole" Baillie singsong. Grace hated

The Watering Hole just for its name alone, how cliche could the owner be?

"Yeah yeah, I need a night out" She wasn't about to get picky with their limited selection in town. Even during the prime season, the pickings were slim, which was part of the small-town charm. There were no extra bars or restaurants that opened just in the summer. What was on the main strip was all she wrote, all year round.

"Yuesss, meet you there at seven!" Baillie exclaimed saying nothing else before clicking off the line.

Grace tossed her phone on the couch, grabbing her laptop and plopping down in the corner of the L shaped sectional. She had a complete view of the shop, track, and beach from this spot. Enveloped in the depths of her computer, she didn't hear the knock on her door, or see Tanner walk into the room.

"No pressure, huh?" Tanner said, awkwardly rubbing the back of his neck. He really needed a haircut; she thought looking at his overgrown locks hanging past his ears. He honestly looked a little green, like the pep talk did the opposite of putting the pep in his step. She thought carefully about what to say to him before responding. She wanted to keep things professional with him, just because they were friends did not mean this streak was acceptable. She had to walk the fine line between friendship and professionalism.

"Winning isn't everything for regular people," she motioned for him to join her on the couch. "But for us it is. Letting this team slip through my fingers would be catastrophic. This is my family name, the first female owner. How would I live with myself if I was the one who sank the ship?" She was being a little dramatic but if it got Tanner to drive better, what's a little melodrama spice. But there was truth in her words. "Maybe the entire town would go under, we are a huge tourist attraction, and bring in a lot of money for the other businesses." She thought about Mrs. Betsy at the Croissant Crossing closing down, she had been in business almost as long as the track. Opening a year after they did, serving as the go to spot the next morning on the way out of town.

"Yea I know Gracie, I've lived here a long time too." They had been friends for many years, but this was the first time their friendship would have to traverse another level where Grace was his boss and their friendship would be put on the backburner. She needed to make that distinction very clear.

"I'll do my very best to not let you down," He stood as he spoke. Making his way towards the door which she was grateful for, she didn't have time for him to be hanging around today.

"That's all I ask T, from anyone, myself, crew, you. No regrets left out on the track."

"No regrets," was all he repeated before knocking twice on her open door then exiting. She really needs to learn how to shut that damn door.

A ping of sadness struck a chord in her chest, turning to face the windows, she glanced out wondering what everyone was doing. Panning her eyes across the track she saw Tanner, he must have just exited the stairwell downstairs to the semi-filled parking lot where Dougie's truck was backed into a spot, her eyes finally landed on her intended target. But to her surprise a pair of dark caramel eyes were already staring back at her. For what felt like an eternity she couldn't breathe, holding his gaze. He quickly winked then looked away. She tried to go back to her computer for the rest of the day, but Grace couldn't get those brown eyes out of her head.

*   *   *   *   *   *   *   *

"I've been looking forward to this all day,"
Grace scream-talked to Baillie who was sitting next to
her. The Watering Hole was packed with locals and
tourists alike, the bass from the speakers pumping some
rockabilly country song. By all means, the place was a
shithole, and absolutely nothing like the bars she had
become accustom too before she decided to move back.
But the old red chairs and booths with sticky floors
brought back memories of her family celebrating many
wins here. The place hasn't changed in fifty years, again
the tourists loved it and they called in charm.

Keen on the local beer and band, everyone
around them seemed to be having a good time either
swaying to the music in their seats or chatting happily
with their companions. It was enough to let Grace take

her mind from work and be in the moment. Grace slammed her drink back and gave Baillie her best 'hello girlfriend, you wanted to drink so let's drink' face.

"I guess we are drinking tonight," Baillie held up her glass in response then slugged the rest of her cocktail down. She looked around hoping to catch the eye of the bartender, which luckily enough she did. Motioning for another round, Grace started to tell Baillie about her day.

"I did catch DW, staring at me through my office window," she fills Baillie in, "But my eyes were already looking for him," she blushed and admitted, she hated that she was attracted to him. Baillie and Grace laughed a little at the silly nickname they had given Dougie. His initials were really DW, but it reminded the girls of that children's show and DW was the annoying sister. They couldn't help but giggle, the drinks they just slammed added extra fuel to the giggle fire. Grace couldn't help that he was a fine chunk of man. There was absolutely nothing wrong with admiring his physique from afar. Only Baillie had to know, its not like the entire town was listening in on their conversation.

"We should have named him Glass Licker," Baillie giggled, motioning to the bartender for yet another round, they were going to be shitfaced by midnight. "Bet he wants to lick something else too!" Baillies shrill laugh filled the air surrounding their table.

"OMG stop that right now," She playfully smacked her best friend on the arm. "I am his boss; we need to keep it professional." But Grace couldn't help but join in with Baillie's continued laughter.

A waiter appeared with the two cocktails they had wanted and two surprise lemon drop shots. Her favorite. She licked her lips in excitement, the knowing taste of sweet sugar on the rim made her dance in her seat.

"These are from the guys over there," the waiter pointed back towards the other side of the bar, where Dougie and Tanner sat.

"What the fuck," both girls said in unison, all dancing stopped. "How long have they been sitting there?" she asked in unison again looking at each other for the answer. Had they overheard any of their conversation? The bar was crowded but Grace knew how voices could carry. Especially if it was a familiar voice and they had been loud. Looking at her best friend with a small, coy smile already on her face, "Well two can play at this game," picking up the lemon drop shot, Grace slammed it back, letting a little drop trail from the corner of her mouth down her chin. Making eye contact with Dougie she licked her lips, as if to say thank you and patted the trail off her chin with a napkin, batting her eyelashes a few extra times for emphasis.

"You ready?" She asked Baillie slurping up the rest of her drink, "I'm suddenly feeling a little too crowded here." She jerked her head in the direction of the guys. She no longer felt like being in the same vicinity as anything that reminded her of work.

"Fuck this place, let's go." Both girls got up, left some money on the table for their tab and walked out into the fresh, salty night air. Grace had to admit, the cool air felt good on her hot neck, the bar seemingly too small upon their exit. That was way more alcohol than she planned on consuming, and she could already feel it hitting her blood stream, each step becoming a little move wavy than the last. She could feel Dougie staring at her as they left, eyes boring in the back of her skull. Why was she even so attracted to him in the first place?

She had always gone after the same type of tall,

dark, and handsome. But Dougie's pull had something different than what she had felt in the past. There was this spark between them that felt like a fire igniting a thousand flames when they were within a few feet of each other. Every conversation lit a spark deep within her core. Did he feel it too?

"This was fun!!! But it reminded me of why I like my couch!!" Baillie giggled and pulled Grace in for a hug, clearly a little more drunk than she wanted to let on. "See you this weekend," she finished before releasing her best friend. She really was the best, every weekend rain or shine Baillie came to the track to support Grace and her family.

Baillie took off in the direction of her house, which was to the right and Grace went to the left to make her way down to her sleepy, little bungalow.

Dougie

Her hips were grinding into his, the contact was electric, making his skin jolt at each touch, every thrust radiating through his body, her body begging him to thrust deeper, he had to concentrate on not coming. He couldn't let this end as quickly as he wanted to devour her. Her pussy was so tight around his throbbing cock, pulsing after each deep push into her tight hole. She was taking it like a champion, tits bouncing in his face, long black hair on either side of her body cascading around her. His balls slamming into her ass, she began to cry out his name.

Dougie's eyes pop open, the loud beeping coming from his phone alarm signaling it was time to get up. Fuckkkk, he groaned, he was clearly not in bed with anyone but himself and his rock-hard shaft in between his legs ... it was only a dream and now he was going to have a raging hard on all day. He never saw her face in his dream, but the hair was a dead giveaway. He had to stop thinking about her.

Tossing his blanket to the other side of his bed, Dougie made his way to the bathroom and turned on the shower. Nothing a hot steam and a wank couldn't fix. Today was a brand-new day to make his bitch, which was a little dramatic, but he needed all the optimism this week.

Sending her that shot should have been his sign to head home that night, he was clearly too drunk to be making smart decisions but nope. The way her tongue ran over her lips and down her chin had been on repeat in his head every moment since.

Dougie and Tanner closed the bar down and now he was most certainly paying for it. What is self-control? The way she licked her lips after spilling a little down her chin. He wanted to grab her right there and lick the sweet lemon vodka from her lips and neck. He had seen Grace in his dreams every night, each ending with a throbbing cock and blue balls. All night he dreamed of her on repeat, any time he would wake up, he would drift off back to the thoughts of her. Her long back silky hair wrapped around his fist. No. He needed to stop this shit right now. He had to stay away from Grace in every way, and keeping their relationship professional was key. Simple yes ma'ams and no ma'ams would have to do, but his dreams were where they could disappear into each other.

Just thinking about avoiding her made his cock hard again. His palm working over his long girthy penis, it didn't feel the same but if he at least found a little relief while he thought about her. Her lips wrapped around the shaft, taking in as much as she can, those pretty green eyes staring up at him, it would be something else. Daydreaming back to his dream this morning, he continued to make long strokes up and down himself until his cock was limp in his hand and the shower water was running lukewarm down his back.

* * * * * * * *

Pulling up to the track, Dougie let out a sigh of relief seeing no other cars in the parking lot. His game of avoidance didn't have to start so soon, he could have a few minutes of peace in the shop by himself. This week was not going to be an easy one either. The night after sending her the shot, Tanner lost another race. Grace had kept her cool while the crew cleared out after the race, but as soon as she thought everyone had left, she went absolutely ape shit in her office. She destroyed a few pillows from her couch with a mail opener and ripped down a couple trophies off the shelf. He watched from the parking lot as her office was the only thing still lit up and he had felt bad for her in the moment, her entire livelihood was dependent on other people, and he certainly knew how that felt.

He couldn't argue and say he wasn't disappointed in himself. He really thought the losses were a one offs, but he couldn't help but wonder if something else was going on in Tanner's head. Was it possible the other drivers levelled up that much during the preseason that they were sweeping his brother under the rug without a second glance?

"Hey Man," Tanner said, breaking Dougie out of his daydream. He had been sitting in the corner of the shop all morning on his laptop going over part orders and race data lost in his own world.

"Is the car good to take out? I want to get a few practice laps in before the storm rolls through,"

"Yea go for," He smiled at his brother, hearing Tanner want to get out on the track made him ecstatic. He clearly wasn't letting the losses get to his head, so neither could Dougie. Tanner yelled across the shop for Miguel to start getting the car ready for the track. For the third time that day a voice interrupted his work, yet again.

"Getting some practice laps in T?" Grace asked in Tanner's direction, but her eyes locked onto Dougie's. What in the world could this woman possibly want from him now? He's had enough torture for one day trying to stay the hell away from her.

"Gotta be on my A game, Gracie-girl," Tanner retorted giving her a sloppy salute and wink before disappearing with Miguel.

Dougie was racking his brain for an excuse to get out of here. It was only noon, but he needed to go and get the fuck away from this intoxicating woman. "Uh I gotta go, last minute dentist appointment," he came up with out of thin air.

"Alright, I didn't know you had…" but he cut her off before she could finish.

"Happened at breakfast, chipped my back tooth. It's killing me," he cupped his cheek in pain however he doubted it was convincing. "I gotta go. Twelve thirty appointment," He finished. Slamming his laptop shut and disappearing out the shop doors. Seriously? He thought to himself, hopping into his truck. A dentist appointment was the best he could have come up with. He was going to have to drive into the city to make this look legit. So much for a peaceful day at work.

Fuck.

* * * * * * * *

"Sooo, are you avoiding me or is it just coincidence that you just happen to be jogging out of every room I enter?"

Her voice breaking through his thoughts yet again. He had been sitting at the bar at The Watering Hole for over an hour nursing the same, now warm beer, but he was too lost in his own thoughts to bother drinking it.

"No Princess, I'm not avoiding you," was all he could get out. He couldn't escape this woman if he tried, she was around every corner.

Whatever this spark between them was, it was scaring the shit out of him. There was this invisible magnetic pull that he felt deep within his soul. He wanted to absorb every ounce she was willing to give and pushing her away was tearing his soul apart. She pulled out the stool next to him and made herself comfortable.

"Tequila soda, lots of ice and extra lime," she asked the bartender when he appeared in front of where they were seated. The giant wall behind him filled with every liquor known to man, gently glowing from the inlayed lights. The glow illuminated Graces petite face and Dougie stared at the slope of her nose and the pucker of her juice lips. He made a mental note to remember her drink order this time around instead of having to phone a friend, like a fool.

"Sure, seems like it," she shrugged, taking a sip of her drink. She looked like everything heaven would be described. Moss green pools for eyes that swirled and got brighter as she got more excited and long black hair that looked like velvet shimmering against the light. He couldn't keep his eyes off her and at this point he was ready to give up trying. He secretly thanked god that it was only happy hour, and the bar only had a few patrons.

"How'd you know I was here?" he asked perplexed she had left the track early, she normally stayed late into the night waiting for everyone else to leave. She chuckled taking another sip of her drink, gently brushing a lock of hair out of her face.

"Hmmm I think your big black, lifted pickup truck gave it away." Duh. "Which I was able to see from the parking lot of the track when I went out to my car to get a sweater."

He didn't know what to say to such an obvious answer and felt so dumb for thinking he could hide from her in this small town. He let the gentle lull of the background music fill the silence. Hopefully she would get the hint and leave.

"I think T's going to surprise us this week,"

Nope. She definitely didn't get the hint.

It did catch him off guard by the way she used his brother's nickname. They both called Tanner 'T', but it was weird that they didn't name him T together, but both discovering their likeness for the nickname and learning years later they called him the same thing. He knew T being short for Tanner wasn't original or special, but it still felt weird. Another connection he couldn't ignore.

"What makes you say that?"

"He's doing practice laps without you begging he too," she suggested and shrugged "He also seems less cocky which is hard to believe." Tanner was the type of guy who knew he was good at something and claimed he didn't need to work on the talent. He would tell you, it came naturally and you can't practice being natural.

"That's very true," but unlikely, is what he wanted to finish his statement with, but didn't want to ruin her good mood. Whatever was going on in Tanner's head was about to drop like a bomb, there was no way he could keep this charade up much longer.

"We'll I have high hopes,"

"Don't you always, Princess."

God, he needed to get away from this girl before the wrong head started thinking for him. He couldn't stop staring at her lips when she spoke, the way they were the perfect shade of pink, juicy and eager to be kissed. He imagined nibbling on her bottom lip. He had to make a move to leave. Now. His cock was pressing up against the fly of his jeans, there was no way she wasn't going to see his bulge when he got up. They needed to lower the lights in this fucking place.

He waved the bartender over hoping he could make an exit rather quickly.

"Close us out please," he murmured before throwing a few twenties on the bar. "You can keep the change," he told the kid, getting out of his chair and trying to avoid Grace's gaze at all costs.

"I gotta go, early morning," He told her before breezing past her chair, hand hovering over his crotch trying to cover the hardness that refused to go down no matter what he thought about. Fuck. He shouldn't be leaving her there, but if he left with her, he wouldn't be able to keep his hands off her and once he started there would be no stopping. If he *had* her, it would be forever. He jumped up into his pickup truck and shoved the keys into the ignition, the dashboard came to life and the engine roared as he peeled down Mainstreet, towards his house.

* * * * * * * *

Streamlines of sun broke through the curtains, waking Dougie up early Saturday morning. He needed to remember to get black out shades, he needed at least two more hours of sleep. Staring up at the ceiling, having been unable to avoid Grace at work, he was dreading spending the entire day with her. He tossed and turned all night, finally finding peace in the early hours, he was so not ready for today.

From about eight am to eleven pm they would be at the track stuck with each other. Today was looking out to be no easier than any that had come before. Throwing the covers off him and padding toward the shower, he hoped the ice-cold water would wake him up out of this delusion and hopefully tame his dick for the day.

The easiest part of his morning had been deciding to walk to the track, fresh air would do his mind good. The sun was already high in the sky, but the humidity was low, creating the perfect weather for a cool walk-through town. Grace's father helped Dougie purchase his house over a decade ago when he had been promoted to head mechanic, the position Miguel now held. He couldn't help but think back to him and Jim standing in front of the house, both being too manly to admit it, but before they even saw the inside, they knew that the house would be the one. It had taken him years to pay back Jim, but it would have taken him longer to pay back the bank and it felt really fucking good handing in the last check. Jim had taken him out to dinner that night as a celebration, ordering thick steaks and bourbon. Truthfully Jim was a better father than his own, but it would crush his dad if he ever known that thought passed Dougie's mind.

Main street was mostly quiet as he strolled, the shops not opening for a few hours leaving only the breakfast cafe and Freaky Deeks bustling with tourists ready to take on the beach, or whatever activity they had planned until the race started. It amazed him every year how people planned their entire trips around watching this team race.

Taking a second to look down at the watch on his left wrist, he still had time, why not. Grabbing the handle for Freaky Deeks, Dougie stepped inside. It really felt like taking a step back to the 70's with the loud music and tie dye posters on the walls. Deacon, the owner was just as weird as the shop, but man did he know how to make a good cup of joe. Getting on the small line, he hemmed and hawed over getting Grace a drink. Had she already had her coffee? Does she drink more than one cup per day? Dougie would probably keel over if he didn't have at least two cups per day. These were the types of questions that kept him up at night, dying to know the answers too. He yearned to know everything about her, every fact about her life, ever curve of her body, every version of that perfect smile. He wanted to know it all.

By the time it was his turn, he asked the young girl behind the counter for his usual, black iced coffee, and for Grace's signature iced latte with skim and caramel. The cashier seemed to smile as she took his money. Likely the entire town had seen them at the bar together the other afternoon. They had probably seen him storm out like a child, not like anything even remotely non-kosher happened, but the likelihood of the rumor that Owner and Crew Chief were getting cozy was something he did not need flying around town. It was like the entire town was in on his little itsy-bitsy crush on Grace. Shaking the dirty thoughts of her from his mind, he grabbed their drinks and headed the rest of the way to the track.

Trying to be sly and still avoid his boss, he dropped her coffee off on her desk with a simple post it note that read:

"Happy Race Day!"

Grace

"A hail Mary is what we're calling it" Grace clinked glasses with Baillie before downing the celebratory lemon drop shot that was sent to their table. They went straight to The Watering Hole after Tanner finished his first-place media circus. It was well after midnight, but the party seemed to carry right on over from the track to the bar. Just another way STJRacing kept the little town of Driftwood Bay alive. She had no idea who had sent the shot and she didn't care; everyone here was here to have a good time. The first win of the season felt fucking good.

As much as she loved the good press for her little team, she hated having to physically be a part of it. Especially now as an owner, she's opened herself up to more scrutiny from journalists and social media trolls. Pictures were wanted not only with Tanner and his car but also the new face of racing. Everyone was dying to know what it was like being a woman in racing. Well, it was fucking hard, she thought to herself taking another sip of her tequila soda, looking around the bar. She couldn't let those silly trolls mess with her thoughts, tonight was about their big win, to break the streak, nothing would hold them back. Now they were going to be starting a new streak, a winning one.

"Why do I have a feeling this whole town is talking about me?" she whisper yelled to Baillie a little louder than intended.

"They are stoopid, your team just won," she responded, shaking Graces shoulders as if to wake her up from a deluge "and word on the street is you and Dougie were getting cozy here the other night," a wicked grin spreading across her best friends face.

"OMG THAT'S NOT TRUE!!" This time she was yelling, the people sitting closest to their table really turning to stare this time. "That's not true," she repeated quieter, "We had one drink then he went running out of here as per usual!" she huffed. Annoyed, that whoever started this rumor left out that key part of him leaving her at the bar, by herself.

"He even lied about having a dentist appointment," she stuck out her bottom lip and pouted, sounding and looking like a child who was told no but she didn't really care.

"How do you know he lied?" Bailed asked, her eyebrow skyrocketing to new heights.

"He wasn't in pain! who goes to the dentist for fun? You go if you're in pain and that man was not in pain!" she laughed, and Baillie seemed to nod in agreement.

These guys must have a sixth sense cause as if by magic, a Williams brother was standing in front of them. At least it was Tanner and she was seventy five percent sure he heard none of their conversation.

"Hey Tanner, great win today!!" Baillie stood, giving him a hug.

"We couldn't be prouder T. You scared me there for a few weeks, but you really pulled it off today!" Grace said, scooching over and offering some of the booth for him to sit. Wordlessly he sat, accepting the offer, "So what were you to hens gossiping about when I walked over? One second the entire bar was staring at you, the next you were both in fits," he asked quizzically. Shit, so maybe he had heard them gossiping about his brother.

Dougie was a fine piece of man that she daydreamed about once or twice, but she could never actually touch. Tanner and Grace had developed a better friendship over the last few weeks, her goal with the team had always been to be hands on with every aspect but spending a few days out on the track with Tanner seemed to greatly improve their chances of winning this season.

She had spotted Dougie lurking those days, somewhere about the shop working on some meaningless tasks that made him too busy to join them, but whenever Grace went to scope out where he was, he would already be looking at her as if his eyes were glued to her silhouette.

"We were actually talking about Dougie," Baillie said enthusiastically as Grace stomped on her foot under the table. A small ooooww came from Baillie's side of the booth. "He's been avoiding Grace." She continued, not heading Grace's foot stomp warning.

"He has become the butt of our jokes," Tanner laughed, elbowing Grace in the ribs as if to join in laughing at Dougie's expense. He had become the butt of their jokes with all his sulking. But she wasn't enjoying the conversation one bit.

"That's mostly you," Grace admitted not looking either of her table members in the eye. "Speak of the devil." she finished. These guys had a sixth sense, there is no way he would just appear like that.

"Hey look who it is!" Baillie basically exploded

from her seat, we needed to get her water the next time the waiter made an appearance. "I got a question for you?"

"Shoot." Dougie said to her as he slid in the booth across from Tanner his eyes never leaving Grace.

"Why are you avoiding Grace?" she asked, the entire table could tell how giddy she was to ask that question.

"Jesus Christ," he sighed, "I am not avoiding you."

"Oh yes you were," Baillie started talking over Grace again, "Gracie said you lied about your dentist appointment last week?" Baillie swirled the straw in her drink just like she was stirring the pot.

An eyebrow of his shot up, "Oh she thinks I lied??" Dougie turned fully to Baillie as if this was life or death.

"why are we talking about me in third person, I'm right here?!" Grace spoke, to seemingly no one. Clearly Baillie and Dougie no longer remembering she was there.

"I would never lie to you, Princess." his eyes coming back, locking onto hers. Instead of the usual deep brown, the warm lights of the bar cast caramel shadows across his irises that made them sparkle like stars in the sky. He took a long swig from his beer before saying "I would love to play twenty questions with you ladies, but I really walked over here to round up my brother. Big win but he better rest up." He stood from his side of the booth motioning for Tanner to finish his drink and do the same.

"Goodnight Princess," he said, locking eyes with her momentarily before turning and saying goodnight to

Baillie. Tanner merely waved from behind his big brother's shadow knowing better than to argue about leaving.

Both ladies finished up their drinks and escaped outside. Looking down at her watch it was nearly three am. No wonder she felt like she had gotten hit by a bus. There was no way she would be making it to the track by eight am tomorrow morning, she needed to sleep. Or maybe fall into a coma and never see Dougie again. That was downright embarrassing.

"That man is into you and way over his head. They way he called you Princess, and not in the rich bitch, condescending way," Baillie screeched, "but in the 'I want to take you now, let me bend you over this very table' way!!"

"No, no that's not the case. He has called me princess since day one. He thinks I'm a spoiled princess, in an ivory castle." He motion back toward the shop and track that were just in view. Their white shape outlined against the dark sky.

"A hundred bucks says you're wrong!"

"You're on"

"I give it a few more weeks," Baillie says smiling as she turned to start walking in the direction of her house. It slightly annoyed Grace that her best friend couldn't have picked a house to buy on the same street.

"You don't know anything!!!" Grace called after her best friend who just waved her hand above her head in acknowledgement. Grace's head was fuzzy, and she needed sleep.

Dougie

Winning two weeks in a row was something Dougie could get used too. It felt good, it felt right, it felt like things were going back to the way they used to be. The team fell into a rhythm and boom another first place win for the season in the bag. Cleaning up the little faux paus at the beginning of the season would be easy. Tanner had been racing at his best. Each week beating the previous lap times of his competitors. Which was downright impressive. The kid was putting in the work, and he hoped their father would be proud of his sons.

Dougie was focused on analyzing their output data from last week's race when the familiar click clacks of heels echoed through the shop. He couldn't help but smile, but only slightly. He was in a good mood today and the idea of sparing with his little vixen made his cock twitch.

"Whatcha got there?" she questioned, placing a hand on his shoulder, leaning in to see what was on his computer screen. Her perfume immediately filled his nose with honeysuckle and coconut, this chick literally smelled like summer, and it was intoxicating. He couldn't think straight.

"Good thing it wasn't porn!" he joked, not like he would ever do that at work. But she made him nervous. What the fuck kind of joke was that?!

"You would watch porn in here? Jeez, at least do everyone a favor and go to the bathroom," she laughed, snapping a quick one right back. He loved how quick she was with a joke, almost like a game. He would do anything just to see that heart stopping smile come across her face.

"Just race data from last week," he shrugged his shoulders trying his best to act casual even though her hand on his shoulder was sending sparks throughout his entire body. Her thought brought every nerve ending to life.

"I hope he can keep this streak up, we are doing great," She squeezed his shoulder once more. Finally daring to drag his eyes away from the screen and look at her. She was stunning- her golden skin, with just a touch of pink from being out in the sun too long and a megawatt smile that could light up the room.

Fuck. He was entirely, completely, screwed.

"I know how important this is," he murmured, reaching out to tuck a long piece of hair that had fallen in front of her eyes back behind her ear. Her eyes meeting his, her breath hitched in her throat. Wishing the moment could go for just a second longer.

"I should get back to work, I need to get the guys together once I finish up going through this," his head nodding back toward the laptop. He swore he saw her smile falter, but only for half a second before switching back to her usual megawatt.

"Best we both get back to work," she looked around and clapped her hands, "Busy week ahead!" she spun on her heel and walked back the way she came.

Slumping back into his chair Dougie let out a heavy sigh and put his head in his hands. He watched her movements around the track the rest of the day, careful not to let himself get too close or make it obvious he was escaping her presence when necessary. Clearly they noticed when he was trying to avoid her.

"Hiding from her, isn't going to fix your little problem." Dougie launched off his chair becoming basically airborne from his latest hiding spot, tucked behind an old race car.

"What. The . Fuck. Tanner."

Tanner chuckled at his brother's discomfort, "You clearly do have a problem if you jumped that high." His face going straight, all signs of humor gone, "And whatever it is, you need to fucking kill it." He pointed a finger into Dougie's chest. The men were similar, but Tanner was built for a race car- tall and slender limbs, well-toned and maybe two hundred pounds. He ate clean and worked out regularly. Dougie had the same tall frame, but he didn't have to worry about fitting into the seat of a race car. In the off season, Dougie tore up the gym and any adrenaline filled activity, that would get the blood surging through his veins. No, he was not an adrenaline junkie, he just liked to sweat hard. He was not scared of his little brother, but he feared what his little brother would do if he found out about his crush. Tanner had a rage deep within him that when unleashed, could be deadly.

"I have no idea what you're talking about." He got up from his chair to be eye level with his brother, "Seriously dude." Dougie tried but Tanner simply shook his head.

"You may have had my back all those years, but now it's time for me to have yours and I'm telling you this shit is going to end us." He was waving a finger between Dougie and the general vicinity of the offices. "The haves," he continued pointing directly at the offices, "do not co-mingle with the have nots" he finished pointing between the two of them.

"That's rich coming from you," Dougie scoffed. "How many hours have you spent on the track with her?" His voice only raising a hair but dripped in jealousy. "How much money has lined our pockets from racing. Your sports car that you daily is worth 80k that you bought in cash. I wouldn't call us the have nots."

"But we aren't from the same world, we do the job. They watch the job and sign the checks." Dougie all but rolled his eyes. His brother had a point, but this family wasn't like that.

"I don't want to fuck her!" Tanner practically screamed. "Don't you see the fucking difference brother?" his voice calming down ever so slightly. "Clear this shit up by the weekend or I'm out."

Tanner gave Dougie one last, disgusted look before turning his back and walking towards the parking lot. A few guys around the shop had looked in their direction during their not-so-subtle argument, but no one asked further questions. His brother did have a point, Dougie had spent more time this week running from Grace than actually getting his work done.

Alright, he thought to himself, let's make a list of all the reasons Grace should be off limits. Humming along to the rock station playing in the background Dougie wandered his way from the shop into the team's makeshift kitchenette. It had all the necessities for a group of guys who liked coffee and take out- a few tables spread around with couches for extra seating, a little counter with a sink and a fridge. It was simple and it was all they needed. Most importantly the couches were comfy. Plopping down on the comfiest couch, he opened the notes app in his phone.

1. Tanner

That was an excellent reason. His brother's opinion

mattered most to him. They were a team, a package, a duo.

2. Racing = livelihood

Would he risk his career for a woman? It wouldn't be the first time in history, but would the racing world take him seriously if they found out he fucked his boss? Would everyone assume that's how he stayed on after all of Tanner's losses?

He started to type the 3 but couldn't think of anything. There were only two reasons stopping him from starting something that could completely change his life.

"You look comfy," the voice said, breaking the silence of the room.

"Why the fuck is everyone in this damn building sneaking up on me today," he yelled a little louder than intended. Clearly startled by the intruder. He had made himself comfortable on the couch not expecting anyone else to be around. Tuesdays were most of the crew members' day off.

"Jumpy much?" Grace joked, smiling at him, and plonking down next to him. The cutest umpf left her mouth as she contacted the couch. "Not as comfy as the one in my office but this isn't half badd. I've never sat and stayed in here before."
He couldn't help but chuckle.

"So was it porn," she nudged the arm that was holding his phone.

"No." he said dryly. Clicking off his screen, not risking her seeing what he had actually been up too.

"Cmon, I'm only playinggg," she tried, dragging out the g "I wont tell the boss."

"If you must know, it was racing data. My ass got sick of that hard stool." he lied.

"Fair enough," she gave up easier than expected but she seemed just as spent as he felt. Her head laid back against the cushion, eyes closed. He couldn't help but stare at her perfect, pouty lips and how pretty she looked.

"Fuck this" he said outloud.

"What" was all she got out before he was pulling her into him. His mouth crashed into hers, hungrily waiting for her to let his tongue slide between her lips. He guided her legs down on each side of his muscular thighs. The smell of her honeysuckle and coconut perfume engulfing them once more. Her hips rocked against his and her tongue swirled his. Letting his tongue explore the depths of her mouth, intertwining with hers. A small moan escaped from her lips, he wrapped her long hair around his fist and tilted her head back so he could kiss her neck.

"I hope this is okay," he whispered.

"this is more than okay," she moaned.

He pulled away from her neck and looked her right in the eyes, "If you don't want this tell me now. I won't be able to stop this once we start." Her breath hitched in her throat.

"Don't stop." Was all she said before he claimed her mouth once more.

His dick throbbing beneath her lap. She could feel how hard he was. She swiped his bottom lip with her tongue and started rocking her hips against his lap. Man did he want to get her naked and savior each sound that left her precious lips. It was taking everything in him not to come from her dry humping him. He could only imagine how wet her little panties must be.

Testing the waters, he slipped a hand under her shirt and felt his way along her soft skin to her breast. Her barely their bra was hardly containing her rock hard nipple, it stretched against the thin fabric yearning to be set free. He moved the fabric to the side, and he rolled her diamond peak between his thumb and index finger.

"Oh my god" she moaned, grinding her hips back down into his lap. She was panting against his shoulder, passion sparking between them. He needed to control himself or he was going to bust in his jeans which would not be the impression he was going for. He couldn't wrap his mind around the fact that this beautiful creature was wrapped around his arms. He kissed her hard, tongues meeting, swirling together as one, before pulling away.

"I've been wanting to do that all day." He whispered into her neck, breathing in the sweet smell of her hair.

Grace

Kissing him was electric, her tongue danced against his like they belong together. A single dance they both knew without being taught. The melody banging in her chest, in rhythm with her already pounding heart. He swiped his tongue up and down her neck, kissing just below her ear, sending shivers down her spine. She could feel every gentle sweep of his skin against hers. Just sweet passion and she didn't want it to stop. Her feelings for Dougie were starting to become overwhelming and the fear of missing out on something that could be so good seemed silly. Tanner would just have to get over it. They were all grown adults and there was no reason his childish antics.

"Then don't stop," she whispered as he pulled her mouth back against his, shaking any work thoughts from her mind, the only place she wanted to be was right here, right now, with him.

He already had one hand up her shirt and she swore to herself that was as far as she'd let it go. They were still in the shop, though empty for the night, they shouldn't be risking it this much.

But he kept teasing her left nipple with his fingers, rolling it back and forth sending shock waves through her entire body, pushing her limits further after each wave of pleasure. They could not have sex on this couch, but my god he felt huge between her legs.

Carefully releasing her hair from his other hand, he slid his hand down the front of her pants. His index finger immediately found her clitoris. She released a moan louder than intended, grabbing her free hand, he brought it up to her mouth to help stifle the moans leaving her lips, her other hand keeping herself steady on his shoulder. Waves of pleasure crashed around her as her hips moved against his hand. She couldn't remember the last time she had kissed someone like this, his tongue encircling what seemed like her entire mouth. She loved every second of it. Each swirl of his finger brought her closer to climax.

"Does that feel good baby," he murmured into her neck, his index finger still swirling her clit. "I want you to come for me princess," he circled once more than dipped a finger between her lips and into her wetness. She was soaking wet for him.

"You're so wet for me baby," he whispered against her neck, sending shivers down her spine. Her back arched, feeling his thick fingers inside of her. It's been a few months since her last partner, leaving her extremely tight and sensitive. Her vibrator would no longer serve her justice after being with this man. His fingers stretched her as he added a second and then a third. She could feel the pulsing start at the base of her spine, knowing her climax was near, she swirled her hips feverously against his palm.

She could barely contain herself, his fingers moved fast inside her, pulsing against her g spot. She could feel how hard he was for her beneath her ass.

"I'm going to come," she whispered against the hand covering her mouth as Dougie refused to let up. Her body shaking from the waves of orgasm that continued to rack through her body as he continued to circle her clit. She begged him to stop and her body relaxed against his chest. He slid his fingers out slowly, instantly leaving her feeling empty. She wanted more.

"I can't believe we just did that," she mumbled, lifting her head from his shoulder, looking around the breakroom. Everyone had been long gone since she first wandered in here, but she couldn't help but worry. She took deep breaths trying to calm her ever beating heart that was going about a mile a minute. She could feel his heart beating just as fast under his thin black t-shirt.

Surprisingly he tilted her face to meet his "I can't wait to do that again except for real this time." he growled.

"For real?" she questioned. "That wasn't real?"

"Oh baby, I'm just getting started." his lips locking with hers again, but a faint sound made her heart still. Footsteps. It sounded like someone was walking away.

"Did you hear that?" she asked him, jumping up

from his lap and walking over to the doorway, her eyes wide like saucers. She managed to briefly fix her shirt incase someone was standing near by. Not that it would have helped. Whomever could have been there would have gotten a pretty good show.

Dougie came up behind her, spooking her slightly and whispering in her ear, "I didn't hear a thing. No one is here, Princess." He grabbed her arm and spun her around so that she was facing him.

"No one saw us, don't worry." He brought his arm up to her face and brushed some of the stray hairs out of her face.

Glancing down at her watch she checked the time, quarter to midnight. Holy shit, no one should have been walking around. He was right and she was going to believe him. Out of sight, out of mind. Somehow convincing herself she had been hearing things and she turned back to look at Dougie who hand made himself comfortable on the couch.

"If anything, it was Miguel's kid that cleans at night. He wears headphones and doesn't hear shit." Dougie chuckled, "No one heard you yelling my name."

"I didn't yell your name!!" she yelled jokingly, turning a bright shade of pink. "We should get going, anyway. It's late and we both have to be back here bright and early." she finished looking around the room at what she should grab to take home with her. "Sometimes I swear I should just move in."

Shuffling over to the couch she started grabbing her laptop and papers, getting lost in her thoughts as she cleaned up the space for the next day around where Dougie sat. He kept glancing at her curiously, catching her eye every few moments, offering a small smile, but he didn't say anything. She wasn't a neat freak per say, but she hated nothing more than walking into a mess from the night before and she meant that for anywhere. Her house, the office, the shop, anywhere that could be tidied would...by her.

"Alrighty that will do for now, you ready?" she questioned as she spun and surveyed the space. It looked pretty good for her quick ten minute clean. He stood wordlessly and took five steps to close the gap between them, grabbing her face with both of his large hands and started kissing her once more. Before it could start all over, he was pulling away.

"Let's go before you turn into a pumpkin" he laughed, guiding her out of the office with his hand on the small of her back. It felt natural for them to leave together. She had never really thought of having a partner that lived in the same world she did. She had dated guys in college, but they never seemed interested in what really got Grace excited. None of them had ever been interested in Nascar, that was for sure.

"Well, I am certainly no Cinderella, and I don't have a fairy godmother either," she teased him back.

With all the excitement that had gone on during the day, during their quick walk to the surface lot, Grace had forgotten a key part. Which Dougie discovered when the only car left in the lot was his black pickup truck.

"Were you ever planning on telling me you walked to work?" he chuckled, smoothing a palm over his scruff. "Hop in, I'll give you a no strings attached ride," as if he had read her mind.

She didn't want to have to suffer through the awkwardness of should I invite him in or not. She wanted to jump his fucking bones after that orgasm. But as much as she wanted to drag him by the collar, she needed to close her eyes and gain some much-needed clarity on this entire situation.

He jogged in front of her, opening the passenger

door for her to hop in. The truck was surprisingly clean and smelt like those black ice tree fresheners all the guys used in high school. She smiled to herself, thinking some things must not change. The driver's door opened breaking the silence of the truck, Dougie jumped in on his side and started the massive thing. How did he drive this every day? Its huge for a 10 mile town.

"This thing is huge," she said craning her head to look around the back and bed.

"Yea you'll be saying that later about something else too," he chuckled, and she stilled. His dick was huge, she felt it through his jeans in the break room and man was he hung like a horse.

"What happened to no strings attached?" she asked suddenly questioning if she should tuck and roll out of the door. She may be better off walking.

"Oh god no," he said, grabbing the back on his

neck while he pulled out of the lot, "I didn't mean like tonight or soon or oh god," he groaned "I made a bad joke. Later as in eventually" he clearly looked upset, and she couldn't let him torture himself much longer.

A smile tore across her lips, "Ah just fucking with you." she laughed, playfully pushing her arm into his across the center console. The darkness of the cab kept almost everything cloaked in darkness, invisible to the eye she could just make out the corners of lips turning upwards.

"You got me there; I thought I fucked up. Left, or right?" he asked, pointing in the directions as he said it. "To the right," she responded, wondering where he lived in proximity to her.

"Sweet me too," he answered as if reading her mind once again. They drove the five minutes in silence before he pointed to Gully Lane and said, "I live down that street."

"Oh wow, we are really close, I'm sixteen Pelican," which was only two streets over from his Gully Lane. She smiled to herself, enjoying the idea of them living so close to each other. Before she knew it, their quick ride was ending as he pulled into her driveway behind her black sedan.

"You should swing by my place sometime and see how similar our places are, from the outside they look pretty identical!" he said smiling at her. "Mine could use a woman's decorating skills thought," he teased, "It's been called a bachelor pad a time or two by your grandmother, when she's stopped by to visit" he laughed. Grace had forgotten that her grandparents were very fond of Dougie. He often helped them out with odds and ends around their house, when he was younger, and her father was still in charge.

She liked the idea of seeing his place, what his

bachelor lifestyle could look like. Most certainly different from her calm and cozy abode. She kept her bungalow simply decorated with light colors and fabrics, to mimic the beach, much like her office.

"Thanks for the ride," She said quickly and smiled before kissing his left cheek, then opening the truck door to make her escape before she made any more reckless decisions.

"See you tomorrow," he called after her. She made her way up the front steps quickly before she could change her mind about inviting him in. Unlocking the door at record speed, she turned around to give him a quick wave goodbye expecting him to be backing out but nope, he sat their parked, waiting for her. He waved then shooed her inside as if his truck would not move out of park until she was locked, safe inside the house.

* * * * * * * *

The cat suddenly became the mouse. Grace spent the rest of her week holed up in her office, peeking around corners to make sure hallways were empty, coming in extra early, and remembering to shut the door. Only coming down for brief interludes when she knew Dougie would be elbows deep in a project, unable to step away. It wasn't like she was stalking him or knew his location. Okay maybe she was but it was working.

* * * * * * * *

Grace woke up Saturday morning feeling ready for the day ahead, which was unusual as Saturdays had become her least favorite day. The winning streak they were on really had her going.

"It's got to be around here somewhere…" she said to no one, stretching out and reaching underneath her pillows trying to find her phone.

She had forgotten to plug it in last night, but she

barely used it and doubted anyone would have tried to get in touch with her while she was fast asleep. That's the one thing she truly loved about this town, if someone needed her, they would find her at the track or at her house. There were no stupid missed calls or unanswered texts. People here just spoke to one another, well minus the teenagers- the younger kids are still running through town, eyes glued to their phones.

She did have a habit of checking the weather every morning, and today they were calling for sunny and eighty-five, perfect racing weather. She tossed her green duvet off to the other side with excitement for the day ahead. The sun was shining bright, there wasn't a cloud in the gorgeous blue sky. If this race was going to be anything like the last few, she really had nothing to worry about, but she was going to cross her fingers just in case.

*　　*　　*　　*　　*　　*　　*　　*

The rest of her morning continued to be cheery and bright, much like her personality, her extra good mood spewing out in all directions. Grace had even decided to walk to work, passing neighbors and friends on her way. Some calling out 'good luck' or 'perfect day for a race' as she passed. The buzz amongst the town was electrifying, everyone was ready to see Tanner win again. Herself included.

*   *   *   *   *   *   *   *

The race started off quick, cars manuverhing around each other to solidify their place in the pack immediately. Tanner found his spot in sixth place and held on to it tight. She wasn't too worried about his positioning just yet. There were plenty of laps to go which gave him ample time to slowly move up the ranks to first.

"It's not always about beating them right out of

the gate, you have to remember its also a long haul," her dads voice appeared in her head, reminding her to stay calm. If anything, that man had a way with getting motivational moments to stick in your head. He must have told Grace that line over a hundred times.

Tanner was still holding on to that number six position, unable to get ahead. He had been holding steady, fighting off anyone who tried to take him place and push him back. But the five cars in front of him were relentless.

Only ten laps to go, she thought to herself, eyes wandering around through their little crowd. She had done a good job of avoiding Dougie for most of the day, only interacting when required by the race and he kept his distance to the complete opposite side of the trailer today.

When her eyes finally went back to the track, Tanner had made his way up to second place, only a few inches behind the number thirty-one who was currently holding steady in first place. They cars flying down the straight away into the last turn, Tanner on the inside, closest to the middle of the track, still a few inches behind thirty-one. He was going to need to punch it around this turn and overtake thirty one in the straight away. It was nose to nose. Inches would be separating the win, it would be a picture perfect photo finish. The crowd would eat it up. She was starting to get excited, standing on the balls of her toes, craning her neck to get the best possible angle of their win.

Instead of continuing the with curve, the other cars start to overtake her number five car as it sputtered and slowed to a complete stop in the middle of the track. Just like that the trophy and prize money disappeared from Grace's eyes and red hot rage filled its place.

"WHAT IN THE FUCK WAS THAT!!!" she

yelled, not caring who heard here. Of course causing everyone around her to turn and she didn't care. She found Dougie amongst the crew, and grabbed him by the arm.

"GO FIGURE OUT WHAT THE FUCK JUST HAPPENED!" she fumed and pointed at the stupid race car sitting in the middle of the track, still motionless. Dougie unphased by her attitude, disappeared to figure out what happened. He didn't seem to have a bloody clue either.

Dougie

Excitement bubbled in his chest, no man should be this happy, Dougie thought to himself as he drove into work. It had been raining nonstop since the race on Saturday, as if Driftwood Bay had been mourning the loss with the team. But no amount of rain could ruin his mood.

Pulling into a spot right in front of Deek's, he put the truck in park and dashed inside. To his surprise Deacon was running the register instead of the usual high schoolers.

"Hey Man, good to see ya!"

"Same here! I feel like I'm never up front when you stop in. What can I get ya?" Deeks asked. The guys had gone to high school together, never in the same friend group but always friendly. Dougie may have a permanent scowl; he didn't hate everyone, especially those who supported his coffee habit.

"Black iced with a couple sugars and an iced latte with skim and a pump of caramel." he responded to Deeks handing over a twenty-dollar bill.

"Nah man its on the house, you need it more than me." He chucked and raised his eyebrows at Dougie.

"It was a tough one for sure. I appreciate it."

"You got it, give me a few," and he spun around to get to work on the coffees. When Dougie was sure Deacon wasn't looking, he shoved the twenty in the tip jar.

His eyes wandered around the shop while he waited, letting his mind drift to Grace and the night they had in the breakroom. That was nearly the hottest thing he had ever done with a woman, just thinking of the thrill had his heart, and his cock, pumping with blood again.

"DOUGIE" Deeks yelled out, jolting Dougie from his thoughts. Looking around he realized he was the only person in the shop, as it was still early. "Dude, it's just me." he motioned around the empty room. Deeks just laughed and went back to cleaning up the back bar.

*   *   *   *   *   *   *   *

With each step up the stairs to Grace's office,

Dougie's excitement grew. He was genuinely looking forward to putting a smile on her gorgeous face. When she smiled, the corners of her eyes turned upward and the green of her irises seemed to shine brighter. He knocked on her open office door, surprised at what he saw when he looked around. It looked like a bomb had gone off, papers scattered and half-filled cups littered almost every surface. Had she slept here??

"No, I haven't left yet," she said, having yet to look up from the laptop sitting on her lap. Her eyes seemingly glued to the screen.

"Brought you something," he smiled walking the coffee over to where she was sitting.

"You're amazing," she beamed at him. "I could kiss you right now."

Unable to control his mind, he bent down and kissed her softly on the lips, only letting himself get lost in her for a few seconds. There was nothing she could ask for that he would deny. He was in over his head and needed to come up for air. There was no way she could want this the same way he does. A soft smile spread across her lips, fading the worry from his mind.

"I'll be in the shop if you need me," he whispered in her ear before turning to leave her with her mess. He was surprised she let the disaster zone get this bad. Normally she was a total neat freak.

He could tell she was starting to crack from the loss.

They had been sneaking secret moments all over the track since the night in the breakroom distracting them from what had been a heartbreaking race.

In between appointments and meetings, she would find him in the shop and pull him away, his soul spinning each time she led him into a corner and pressed her body into his. Her lips were always soft and tasted like sweet vanilla. Each secret moment made him crave more of her, but he hadn't let himself fully lose control in her. If he lost control, he was scared he would never get it back.

He was also utterly convinced the shop was haunted and there was absolutely no way he would be making love to anyone on haunted dirt.

Her great grandfather was probably wreaking havoc around the track on his horse and buggy. Okay horse and buggy is a bit of a stretch, but he thought about how different race cars were back then compared to all the technology they had now. The cars were completely fitted with the latest gear, which put them leaps and bounds ahead of where they were all those years ago.

He was lucky to work in such an incredible shop with top-of-the-line products from the sponsorships the team received. He even benefited from the sponsorships;

his Snap On tool collection was immense.

* * * * * * * *

The stress in the shop was high and Tanner's loss last week was a huge blow to the team, and their standings. This place was a ticking time bomb just waiting to explode. The tension in the air needed an industrial knife almost too thick to cut.

"Have you figured out why this hunk of junk suddenly stopped running mid race?" Tanner questioned Dougie, "I had my foot on the gas and then…"

"… and then all of the sudden nothing was happening. Yes, we have gone over this a hundred times. I understand what happened from your point of view." Dougie finished for his brother. They really had had the play by play at least a hundred times. But there was still something nagging at the back of his mind. There was no reason for the car to come to a rolling stop. No spark plugs were missing or damaged, the fuel line was fully intact with plenty of gas left from his last pit stop. Dougie had spent hours the night before reviewing the data with Grace, up in her office stealing kisses between pages of analytics, but he hadn't been able to come up with a reasonable solution as to why the car suddenly stalled. And seriously? Did he hear his brother correctly?

"I'm sorry hunk of junk?" Dougie questioned, his brows coming seriously close together they were on the verge of becoming one, trying to contain his rage. What a no good, entitled brat his brother had become.

"No other race cars suddenly stopped. So yeah, I would call this one a hunk of junk" Tanner bit back, his tone snarkier than it should have been "It's a hunk of junk if it just stops running."

"Did you ever think it could have been driver error??" he seethed, there was no way Tanner would do that, there was obviously something Dougie had missed.

He planned on giving the car an entire look over this week before the race to make sure everything was absolutely perfect. But it felt good to finally say something to get under his brother's skin. Tanner was constantly slinging insults his way and for once Dougie had the upper hand.

"How fucking dare, you!" Tanner roared, pointing a finger at Dougie's face. Both men were equally match but Dougie stood taller than Tanner and had to look down on him a bit. "You're the crew chief, and engineer extraordinaire, this is your fucking problem and your fucking fault! I saw you all smug before I walked up. Flipping through your paperwork, smiling because the only possible answer could be me, the little brother fucking up once again! This is your fucking problem!" His brother was on a rampage now, and once Tanner started, it was hard to get him to calm down.

Seeing his brother like this sent him straight back to their childhood. Watching his mother and father scream at each other in the kitchen of their shitty, brown home.

"No one is accusing you of anything T," he tried to calm his brother down but instead he turned a deeper shade of red.

"Go fuck yourself Doug." Tanner spat, spinning on his heels surveying the room as if he was talking to everyone "There is no fucking race, without me. I don't see another driver lapping me on the track." and he walked off without another word. He was completely out of sight but Dougie could still hear his brother's truck door slam and tires peel out of the parking lot. Well, that couldn't have gone better if he tried. What a fucking joke. He silently thanked whatever god had kept Grace in her office for the outburst. She would had ended his season on the spot, she had made it clear that there would be no disrespect and Tanner just shit all over her legacy.

"You good, my guy?" Miguel squeezed his shoulder, breaking him from his thoughts.

"Yea I'm fine," he responded to his friend but not really believing it himself. "He just needs a few days to cool off, you know how he can be." Miguel had been one of the long-standing crew members that had been with the team from the very beginning. He had watched Dougie grow and supported Tanner driving during his beginning seasons.

"Oh yea, we do. But I thought those days were behind him. I haven't seen that version of Tanner in a long time." There was a hint of sadness in Miguel's voice, like he had just watched his child completely regress into behaviors that had long been forgotten.

Miguel had worked alongside Dougie for the better half of the last decade and they had become pretty decent friends. They were at separate points in their lives, Miguel having a wife and family at home. But they connected about racing on a deeper level and shortly after they had become friends, Miguel opened about how the St. James had helped him to get a footing in Driftwood Bay. He came to Driftwood Bay looking for work one summer and never left. This place had a way of capturing people, in the best way possible. Dougie would only admit it if you asked, but this was his favorite place in the world.

Another voice broke the silence, but it wasn't someone who had just witnessed Tanner's temper tantrum as this voice was entirely female. Just not the female he craved to touch.

"You should tell your brother to slow down, he nearly killed me coming out of the parking lot." Baillie chuckled. The petite woman once again appearing out of nowhere. This chick had a habit of popping up on him, it was bewildering. The coffee shop was still a sore spot in his mind. Her loud voice echoing her thoughts about him getting Grace a coffee had echoed through the town for days. Like the shot heard round the world.

"He is a race car driver." Dougie snapped, harsher than he intended. Baillie wasn't at fault for anything, she didn't deserve that. "I'm sorry. We just got into it about the race last weekend, and he stormed off."

Baillie's eyes softened a bit understanding "All good, but if he's driving like that in the lot." she pointed to the parking lot then to the track "He should start driving like that over there." Dougie couldn't help but chuckle. She had a good point.

"I'll mention that to Grace but maybe you should make that suggestion to Tanner," Dougie chuckled humor draining from his face, knowing Tanner would flip if anyone outside of the racing world tried to give him advice. Especially if it was coming from Baillie who had to him had no clue about racing.

"Oh, I bet you would love to go talk to Grace," she gave him a sly smile, "But you can let your brother know that, and I will let Grace know you get all starry eyed any time her name comes up. Funny which, I didn't even bring her name up… you did," she chuckled, smiling growing, ever knowing what was going on between the two of them. It was atrocious being obsessed with a woman whose best friend was attached at the hip. But at least it was one less person he had to hide his feelings from. They were getting larger and harder to hide away.

Grace

"There is trouble in brother paradise." a voice called from the open doorway. Clearly Grace has yet to learn a thing or two about closing her office door. No one seems to be too keen on knocking.

Grace looked up from her desk to see her amazing best friend. This girl always knew how to make Grace smile and she genuinely appreciated their friendship. They had been through countless boyfriends who they won't remember in thirty years and going to college on two separate coasts. Driftwood Bay had brought their friendship back together, both girls fell right back into place with each other like they had spent no time apart at all.

"I brought sustenance," Baillie said, holding up the bag like a kid in kindergarten during show and tell, grin spread wide across her Sunkissed face. "I figured you haven't left in a while, and by the looks of this place, I'm right." Which was clearly evident. The couch had blankets and pillows thrown across it haphazardly and the coffee table was covered in cups and paperwork. It honestly looked like a bomb had gone off.

"It could use a little tidying," Grace smirked at her best friend, standing up from the desk to clear the coffee table so they had a place to eat.

"I think it needs more than that. Are these cushions sanitary??" Baillie joked as she plopped down in between two blanket piles, moving one across her lap. Grace's head whipping around faster than the speed of light itself.

"Hush big mouth," she said to Baillie as she rushed to shut her office door. "Someone might hear you." she finished putting extra emphasis on the hear you. She was still unsettled from the mystery footsteps and even though her and Dougie had been fooling around at work, they had been extra cautious.

"Oh, so there have been more secret hookups since your breakroom breakthrough" Baillie poked.

"No" Grace tried to lie and sat down next to her best friend. Baillie raised a single eyebrow.

"Okay!! Yes, every night this past week we've made out on the couch hours after everyone else had gone home."

"Oh, my fucking god and you're telling me now??" Baillie screeched, Grace's eyes widening at the decibel volume, she halfway considered covering her ears incase another screech escaped her friends lips.

"It's never intended but we start talking and one thing lead to another. But just kissing and grinding like teenagers," she giggled. "He really is so fucking beautiful."

The girlies let out a squeal that most farmers would mistake for pigs, but they continued on their lunch in fits of hysterics.

* * * * * * * *

What a long ass day Grace thought to herself as she slowly cleaned up the mess left in Baillie's wake and frankly the mess that was left in her own wake. Yet again, someone was knocking on her door and the person immediately started speaking. Did anyone get the word privacy?

"You got a second?" Tanner asked wearily. She really needed to start closing that damn door.

"Only a few, I'm about to head out," she responded, still cleaning, there was no reason she couldn't multitask. Cleaning required little brainpower and helped her work through the most difficult decisions in her life. More people should try cleaning while they make a mental pro and con list; its cathartic.

"I'm confident about this next race," He said strongly but then nothing else came from his lips, his expression caught between wanting to say more but not knowing how to say it.

What was he looking for? A pat on the back after a big loss?

"I'm confident in you too." she mustered "There seems to be no issues with the car, so hopefully it is smooth racing from here on out."

"Yes, you're right. I just wanted you to know I'm here and I'm ready."

"Glad to hear it T. I never doubted you." Even though she did doubt him a little bit, that's the last thing he needed to know right now. If Dougie and the rest of the crew were going to give him a hard time with what's been happening, then the least she could do was support him. It was her team after all and they only had one driver.

In theory, she could drive, but these boys aren't ready for that yet. She had yet to figure out what had been tearing the brothers apart. She had heard yelling amongst the brothers the other day and Miguel had said it was just a brotherly spat. But it felt different, stronger, like two bulls locked on each other.

"Thanks Grace," He said softly before leaving her office. She did a quick survey and figured it was good enough. All the trash that may cause problems if left alone had been tossed and it no longer looked like she was sleeping on the couch. Mission accomplished. She glanced out the window hoping to see a familiar black pick-up in the parking lot. She dashed down the stairs and jogged to where Dougie was locking up the garage bay doors.

"We gotta talk about Tanner," she huffed out of breath, she really needed to get back into running once the weather turned for the fall. "Something is up with him?"

"Something is up Grace," Anger seared through each word he spat in her direction. Where was this anger coming from? "He was the reason we lost last week's race and he's hell bent on fucking blaming me. As if I was in the driver seat and took my foot of the fucking gas."

"Is that what you think he did??" Her eyebrows shooting up, concern lacing her words.

"It's the only possible explanation." He spoke rather calmly now. "I gotta go," was all he said before he jumped into his truck and slammed the door all but in her face. There was more than just trouble in paradise between the brothers and she was starting to worry that this sinking ship would bring down her entire career.

Dougie

Slamming his truck door in her face wasn't necessarily the best idea he ever had but his mind was still spinning from Tanner's outburst that afternoon. He knew they were all under a lot of stress, but he couldn't imagine him throwing another race. If anything, Grace was his friend, and she paid the entire team well. He couldn't have maliciously done *this*. If other teams found out about these little stunts that would end both of their careers faster than Tanner could say 'whoops'.

The drive from the lot to his house wasn't nearly enough time to clear his head but he pulled into his driveway. He sat there for a few minutes contemplating what in the hell was going on with that woman. Anytime she spoke to him it was like everything stop firing at once and stupid shows up instead. He shook the embarrassment out of his head and decided to make his way inside for some much-needed sleep. Hopefully tomorrow would be a better day. He was surprised to hear a soft voice once he opened his truck door.

"Hi" was all she said, and he didn't know what to say, because as we know, stupid shows up when Grace is around. This woman made all the words leave his brain the instant her eyes met his.

"Did you follow me home?"

"Well, I do have to pass your street and I walked

to work today so I figured I would stop when I saw your truck in the driveway," he could see the sincerity swirling behind her long dark lashes looking up at him.

"I'm sorry." was all he said before he closed the distance between the two of them, wrapping his arms around her. She smelt so fucking good; it was intoxicating. "I shouldn't have spoken to you like that. As a friend, as a boss, as... whatever this is." he finished and squeezed her tighter. He wanted it to be more, but he had to figure out how to tell her first. He also had to figure out if this was more to her too.

"So, you think he threw the race?" she asked like we were right back into the previous conversation.

"I think so," he shrugged, letting her go to grab her hand and lead her towards the house. "Let's talk about this inside, you know how small towns are." she craned her head around the street to in fact see a number of window curtains move back into place as she did, and a few lights suddenly go dark.

"Good idea," she said looking at him. He led her up the porch steps, unlocking the front door into his quaint little living room. His bungalow was a two bed, one bath that was close enough to the ocean that he could hear the waves crashing into the sandy shores when he couldn't sleep at night. Grace did a quick twirl as if she was surveying the place.

"It's rather cute for a bachelor pad," and she was right, he did try to keep it cute and cozy as a sanctuary away from the madness that came with racing. Dark hardwood floors flowed through the entire house with lots of windows to let in nature light. He couldn't wait to have her over during the day.

"I like peace and quiet when I'm home," he could tell she liked the place the way she dropped effortlessly onto the couch and patted the cushion next to her, motioning for him to sit as if it was her own house.

"The data shows nothing wrong with the car other than lack of fuel to the engine." he started, which she quickly finished with "which would be caused by taking your foot of the gas."

"Exactly." he said facing her on the couch, a worry line creasing against her pretty little forehead. He understood how dangerous a rogue driver could be, not only willing to risk his life on the track but the other drivers as well.

"That's why he came to my office early," she said in mock recognition. "He assumed you spoke with me about this and came in to tell me that he was ready to race this weekend." Her eyes searched for an answer in his that he didn't have. He truthfully had no idea what Tanner was capable of or why he was even doing this.

"I accept your apology by the way," she

switched to the next topic, thank god. This beautiful woman was sitting in his living room talking about his brother.

"Oh you do?" he teased.

"I do, but your punishment will be dealt with at a later date. We need to focus on this" she paused "issue. Before we explore any more of this" her long pointer finger motioning between the two of them. "I can't handle another loss." her voice is softer this time.

"I know, I'll do whatever I can to help." and he meant it. "We will keep encouraging him the rest of the week, a lot of practice in the simulator and it'll all work itself out," he tried to sound as comforting as he could. Hopefully she believed at least half of it.

"You're right," she said, moving closer to his side. Now that business was out of the way she seemed to relax.

"Would you like to get dinner on Sunday night?

He asked her, wrapping an arm around her shoulders.

"Like a date?" she sounded unsure, but her eyes were glued to his with a passion rolling through the emerald pools.

"Yes, like a date." he playfully nudged her. "I know a good spot that's a few towns over, I doubt anyone will see us."

"I'd love that," was all he let her say before meeting his lips with hers. He had been dreaming about kissing her all day. Her lips felt like soft pillows that he could devour for hours. His tongue melded with hers as they explored each other's mouths for what seemed like hours.

"Fuckkk" he groaned as she pulled away, breaking their mouths apart.

"I should go," she whispered, leaving a trail of kisses down his neck to the collar of his shirt.

"I agree but I don't. I want you so badly" he grabbed her face so she could look him in the eyes and understand "But I want to do this right. Messing around has been fun, but this is real." She stopped his words with a kiss right on his lips. He had never had a woman do that before.

"I can't wait for Sunday," was all she said before she got off the couch and grabbed her belongings.

"Can I at least drive you home? Or walk you?" he asked, already knowing her answer.

"It's just a silly small town," she giggled and blushed before walking out his front door.

Jesus Christ that woman would be the death of him. Looking down he saw his dick poking out of his jeans at a weird angle. Has it been like that the whole time?? He looked like a horny thirteen-year-old who got his first woody in class. He brushed a hand over his face trying to scrub away whatever embarrassment had been left and went to the fridge for a much-needed beer.

Grace

"Cheers," Grace spoke as she raised her wineglass to him. Dougie had surprised her with a bouquet of sunflowers when he showed up at 6:30 to pick her up for their dinner reservation. Which just happened to be at one of the nicest steakhouses in the area. We were far enough away from the Bay that no one would likely drift over here, especially on a Sunday night. The number of tourists that had shown up for yesterday's race would no doubt be keeping the locals busy tonight. "That god we have something to celebrate." she finished, taking a long slow pull from the glass. It was a yummy red cabernet with a woody undertone.

The waiter came to take their order and the conversation slipped into a natural give and take. Grace had initially been anxious before, but her nerves calmed easily in his presence, which was something she definitely wasn't used too. Not that her previous relationships were bad or abusive, but she was always chasing her boyfriends at the time to take her out and make her feel special. Those guys usually never lasted and Grace would find herself alone, which she didn't mind. But here was this strong minded, bull of a man pulling out all the stops for her. She felt silly for worrying so much about not having anything to talk about besides racing.

"We should take the bike out for a ride one night," his voice broke through her thoughts. She had been listening to him and engaging back in the conversation with him but her mind was always working double time.

"I haven't been on the back of a bike in years!" She exclaimed excitedly, that's such a good idea and there was no way unwanted eyes would catch them. "It's a date." she said, clinking her glass with his again. Everything about the rest of dinner was delicious and Grace's worries seemed to melt away. They chatted easily about her childhood and what it was like growing up next to the great Jim St. James and Dougie talked about his dad and how spending time with him at the shop led him to right where he was meant to be.

* * * * * * * *

Dougie made a left turn down her street and unwilling to let the night end so soon, she decided to speak up "Do you want to come in for a nightcap?" she asked. What are we 70? A night cap?? She roasted herself internally on that one.

"What are we 65? But yes, I'd love to come in." his laughter filling the truck as he put it in park. His laugh was intoxicating, and he rarely let it out, but oh when Dougie laughed the room felt it.

"I regretted the nightcap, the second I said it," she giggled, unable to control his contagious good mood. Walking up her front steps, she couldn't help but look back and notice how natural his truck looked in her driveway. Before she could get the door fully open after unlocking it, Dougie's hands were around her waist, spinning her so their mouths could meet. His intoxicating cologne filled her nostrils as he continued to explore her mouth with his tongue.

"Is this, okay?" he whispered in her ear before leaving a trail of smooches down the center of her neck. "More than okay," was all she could get out. Breaking apart from the kiss, Grace grabbed his hand to lead him to her bedroom. Thank god she was a neat person and cleaned up the disaster that was trying to pick an outfit for tonight, or there would have been no bed to lay on.

Pulling him down onto the bed with her she straddled his hips and continued to kiss him. Each kiss becoming more intense. His hands traveled from her waist to her breast grabbing each one gently. She could feel how badly he wanted her and she was reveling it.

Dougie

"Should we make Sunday dinners a ritual?" Dougie asked Grace as he bumped hips with her walking towards the track.

"Oh, another date already?" she smirked, "Someone is eager," teasing him, her hand gently grazed his arm, sending shivers down his spine. He couldn't help but imagine those long fingers trailing down his stomach to his cock the other night.

"Why wouldn't I want to take the most beautiful woman out on another date? We'll switch up the restaurant too." He looked at her face to meet her eyes and her green emerald pools were swirling bright. God he wanted to pull her in for a kiss, but he settled on a smile instead. "I'm going to finish getting everything ready. Meet you at the start." deciding last minute a smile wasn't enough he gently reached for her right hand and kissed the bottom of her palm. He'd do anything to make her melt.

On big race days it felt nice to share the same level of anxiety with someone, someone he was developing major feelings for, and that same someone was also his boss and his brother's boss.

"See ya laters," Grace murmured as she turned to go about the rest of her morning.

*   *   *   *   *   *   *   *

Two hours later and the cars were lined up in order, waiting for the start of the race. With Tanner's unusual driving this season, the number five car was sitting in the middle of the pack. Not at all where Dougie saw themselves sitting this year, but it was still recoverable. Everything was recoverable. The loudspeakers crackled as the MC's voice came overhead,

"Drrrriveerrrrs aaaarrreeee youuuuu readddddyyy!!!"

The pack grandstands went absolutely nuts, not only did they have a good MC that kept the crowd engaged during downtimes and flags during the race, but he was also a well known local that drew in his own crowd. The cheering roared from all directions, but not nearly as deafening as the racecars revving their engines at once. It was a feeling that reverberated through your bones.

"Locked and loaded T?" Dougie asked into his headset that was connected to Tanners helmet via bluetooth. Every crew chief had this connection to the driver as a way to coach and help during the race.

"Lets do this," was all that came back from the other end. Within a few moments the yellow flag was out and the pacer car was leading the racecars around the track. The job of the pacer was to take the cars on a lap or two around the track as a quick warm up, then the pacer pulls off and the green flag goes out for the racers to continue on.

Dougie watched Tanner with such intensity that he didn't notice Grace standing next to him until he nearly elbowed her in the face when Tanner overtook the number thirty one car.

"Woah short stuff, sorry I didn't see ya there," she looked amused with a twinkle in her eyes. He didn't know what their path would be but he was totally fucked for this chick.

Very very fucked.

"He's holding strong," she said, equally engrossed in the race as he was. "He just needs to get around that number seventeen car," she pointed out to 11 o'clock as the cars chased each other down the straight away. Dougie stroked a hand through his scruff, damn not only was she beautiful all the time but when she talked about racing at the track, it made his dick twitch even more than usual.

"I don't know what I like more," he bent down so his lips where right next to her ear. "Watching those lips talk about racing or watching those lips wrapped around my cock." a deep red blush creeped up her neck and face.

"Someone might hear that dirty mouth of yours, its almost as dirty as this track" she retorted as she drug a long finger along the top of the nearest work bench, flipping it over to reveal the dust on the pad of her finger.

"Don't worry Princess. No one can hear me." he grabbed her dainty wrist and positioned her infront of himself so she could feel what she did to him.

"Better view," He said to Miguel who happened to make eye-contact with Dougie while he was maneuvering Grace in place. He stood a full foot taller than her, so the view was never the issue. He pushed his rock hard cock gently into her back.

"Seriously" she whipped her head around laughing.

"I can't help it, Princess." was all he said before the telltale sound of metal crashing into metal ripped their eyes from each other. More bangs and screeches followed the initial crash and sirens now filled their eyes with deafening wails.

Grace pushed him towards the track, "Go find out what happened, I'm going up top."

Dougie jogged toward the track entrance from the pits but was stopped by a big security type dude.

"No one past this point sir, only emergency personnel,"

"But one of the drivers is my baby brother," Dougie almost wailed. The security guards' eyes softened momentarily, "I'm sorry my guy, but that's an even bigger reason as to why I can't let you through." Fuck. The guy was right. Running back to their trailer in the pits, Dougie climbed up the ladder that led to the roof. Back in the old days the guys would stand on the trailers to fully watch the race but with today's technology you could watch from the inside of the trailer on a 40-inch flatscreen if you didn't have a direct view.

Grace was already on the roof with Miguel and his son. Her phone was open, in her hand but her gaze was off in the distance watching as their number five car was upside down and on fire. Dougie collapsed to his knees next to her. He felt hands on his shoulders, but he didn't know whose. All he could here was her voice,

"The office doesn't know anything yet, but the second they can get him out, someone is going to come for you to go with him to the hospital. Miguel, Tony can you guys help him down?"

"I don't need help," he gritted through his teeth as he stood, a little wobbly. She reached out to grab his hand, but he pulled away before she could get close enough. If only he had been focused on watching the race instead of the vixen that was in front of him. "I'll see you later," was all he said before he made his way down the ladder and to the track entrance gate to wait patiently to be taken to his brother.

Grace

Grace sat outside the hospital in a parking space, unable to drag herself inside. She had been given updates from the doctors, so she knew what lay ahead of them for the next few months. But going inside was a different story. She was absolutely fucking terrified of what she may actually find inside. She hated hospitals, hell she didn't know a single person who didn't. But for her, hospitals meant death. Every time a loved one had gone into the hospital for whatever reason, they always came back out in a box. She checked her phone one more time hoping for a last-minute escape, or maybe a text from Dougie. He had been radio silent since the race three days ago. Sighing heavily, she hauled herself out of the car and inside.

The room was cold, painfully white, and empty besides Tanner in the bed. He looked peaceful, too bad he was anything but that. He had burns on forty percent of his body from the fire and multiple bone fractures in his legs and pelvis. They were able to repair most of the damage. He wasn't out of the woods yet, but day one compared to day three is looking much better.

"You scared me dude," she whispered as if she would wake him. She sat down in the visitors chair next to his bed and asked God for advice. She wasn't the religious type, but they could use all the extra help they could get. She prayed for her friend and for her team. As she said her amen, the door to Tanner's room swung open with a bang. Dougie stopped dead in his tracks.

"What are you doing here?" he asked with ice in each word.

"Checking on my team," she looked at Tanner then back to Dougie, "Both members."

"You shouldn't be here,"

"Like hell that way my car he was driving under my family name. I care about his fucking wellbeing. I have every right" She stood from her chair and marched right up to Dougie's chest. "Push me away all you want, but I'm not going anywhere." She pushed past his broad shoulder and left Tanners room. Who did he think he was, telling her what to do.

*   *   *   *   *   *   *   *

Back in the safety of her car, she grabbed her phone and

dialed Baillie's number. Baillie had been at the race with her family in the Grandstands, so she was very aware of what had happened.

"No good?" was all her best friend asked.

"No good bails" was all Grace was able to sniffle out.

"Red or white?" Baillie asked.

"Huh"

"Red or white, bitch?!"

"Red, definitely red if you're calling me a bitch already."

"Track or house,"

"Meet me at the track, I have paperwork things to do in my office," she sighed.

"Alright, see you in a few" and her best friend was gone, clicking off the line. She wasn't feeling much better but at least she didn't have to wallow alone.

Picking up her phone one last time, she dialed a

familiar number and backed out of the parking spot.

"Hey Kiddo," her dad's warm, rich voice came through the other end.

"Hey Daddy, you busy?"

"Never for you sweetheart, rough week huh?"

"Who told youuu??" she felt like a child whining, but she honestly wasn't surprised that he knew. When Grace took over her father agreed to stay out of her hair unless she asked, but he never agreed to stop watching the races no matter where in the world his travels led.

"It's all over the racing world bug" he chuckled. "Did you think I wouldn't find out?"

"No that's not it at all," and she meant it. She didn't care that her dad knew she was just surprised.

"Just keep your head up, fix what you're capable of and the rest will fall into place," Her father said, he had been saying this to his kids since before they could walk and he probably told it to a few crew members over the years as well.

"Thanks dad," she knew just hearing his voice would make her feel better. And he was right, she could only fix what she was capable of.

"Welcome kiddo, I gotta jump. I'll see you soon. I love you" was all he said then the line clicked off.

"Love you too," she said back to the dial tone. Thinking about it for a minute, what did he mean by gotta jump? Was he off on one of his hair brained adventure trips? She couldn't be stressed about this now.

Dougie

It had been a couple hours since Dougie so much as kicked Grace out of Tanners hospital room and he was starting to feel the emptiness she had left behind. The stark white walls and floors were starting to close in on him, his mind swirling with the what if's that life laid ahead of him. He would obviously have to take care of Tanner depending on how things went with his recovery.

"Hey" a small voice called out.

"Hey, you're awake," Dougie said as he hit the call button for the nurse. They had kept his brother in a medical coma to help with any brain swelling and pain but they stopped those meds yesterday, so they had been on Tanner's time to wake up.

"We'll Tanner, beside some scars and a long recovery ahead, you'll be back to yourself within the year."

"A YEAR?" Tanner basically screamed. "I still have a race to win next week and another season to start in 5 months!"

"Yes, this type of injury takes time to heal and it's on your body's time. We can't make your recovery go any faster. Rest is key here." The doctor finished and left the room. Clearly wanting to escape his brother's wraith.

"Let me call Grace and give her the good news,

she was here earlier but your condition was still the same as the day previous," he looked over at his brother who was clearly making a face.

"What's the puss for?" Dougie teased.

"Nothing. Nothing." Tanner retorted quickly changing his face from disgust to indifference.

"What's the issue with Grace?" Dougie tried one more time.

"Well, you've certainly changed your tune brother."

"She's trying her best here, isn't that what we expected from her? Nothing to change and to just win? We are supposed to be in this together."

"Yes," He smirked, "She's really doing her best with all those crashes" Tanner finished. It was like a ton of bricks came crashing down on Dougie. Every wreck he and Grace had spent hours poring over the data, trying to find solutions to a problem that only existed in the driver's seat. She was going to have a fucking field day with this news. She had been confused by the lack of findings in the data but she never outright blamed Tanner for the issues.

"You almost got yourself killed over this?" Dougie was pissed. No, he was worse than pissed, he was fucking fuming.

"We are too big for this team," Tanner yelled back, "After our second L, the Langles called me to chat about who I'd be racing for next season." Tanner paused, "and of course my dear brother was also offered a spot."

"Unbelievable" was all he could say. Is this the kid he had raised and groomed for racing?

"That was supposed to be the end of the losing streak once our contracts had been sent over to me. But one night I was at the track late, printing out the documents and I saw two little love birds all over each other on a cute couch in the boss's office." Tanner was smiling now, bigger than the mother fucking Cheshire cat. Grace had been right when she thought she heard footsteps.

"So instead of just leaving her team at the end of the season, you decided to wreck her racecar and her career all in one go?"

"Well brother, I knew you wouldn't come with me if everything was hunky dory over here. You wouldn't have left with me if you were fucking her."

Dougie's mind was racing and he struggled to comprehend the danger his brother put himself in all over a contract. A bloody, fucking contract. What could the Langles have to offer that Grace wouldn't.

"I have one question before I never speak to you again," Dougie asked. For the first time since Tanner woke up he looked uneasy.

"Go for it" Tanner seethed. He had zero right to feel anything other than remorse. His attitude needed a reality check.

"All of this was on purpose," he waved his finger in the air circling. He was disgusted with his brother's behavior and could not for the life of him wrap his head around where the hell brained idea came from. There was no way Tanner could have thought of this scheme on his own. The Langles had to have deep hands in this. There had to be more laid out on the table for Tanner than to just switching teams. Especially if he was losing.

"Not to this extent, I don't want to die racing," his head hung low.

"I have to go," was all Dougie said before exiting his brother's hospital room for the last time. He fully planned on never speaking to his brother again. He should have been keeping a closer eye on how far out of hand Tanner's spiral had gone.

"And go where?" Tanner called after him. But he was already gone.

He had to find Grace.

Grace

"How'd I know you'd be here?" the voice startled her; she looked up from her corner on the couch that she's called home since the accident. Before she could kick him out the same way he kicked her out of Tanner's hospital room, he was already moving toward her at lightening speed. This mountain of a man who could crumble her heart into a million little pieces with a simple goodbye.

"I'm a creature of habit and right now this is the only place I feel like I belong," she whispered. She had been eating herself up over Tanner, the nights turned long and sleepless to the point that she would give up. Pacing around the office or walking around town, trying to figure out what the heck could have happened with that car. The town had been a swirl with rumors of foul play, that was the one she had heard the most. Baillie reminded her each day to ignore the nonsense, but blocking out the noise was easier said than done.

"I'm so sorry," was all he said as he reached out to grab her hands, taking the spot on the couch next to her, kissing both of her palms, "I have so much to tell you, but I don't know where to start." His touch pulled her from the depths of her mind, bringing her back up to the surface for the first painful breath.

"Start at the easiest part" she suggested, it was something her father would have said. She amazed herself in how casual she could sound while absolutely dying on the instead. Her anxiety was gnawing at the back of her skull. She was doing everything to keep from shaking.

"It's all Tanners fault," Dougie spoke slowly, her eyes almost bulged out of her head. Did she hear that correctly?! How could this possibly be Tanner's fault. Not of this magnitude. That would be career suicide and this guy lived, ate and shit racing. This certainly didn't sound like the easiest part of whatever he had to say. This was absolutely crazy. She had never heard of a driver throwing races like this.

"He got an offer from the Langles after the second loss, at the beginning of the season and decided to join them next season." He didn't say anything else but the grimace on his face said it all. What a fucking piece of shit traitor. It took every ounce of her being not to say that out loud, she knew even it would hurt Dougie even though it was his brother causing the shitstorm they were now sitting in the middle of. How dare that shithead come in here and think he could destroy everything her family had built. From the ground up, with his father helping along the way as well. Tanner would be nothing without her family.

"And let me guess, this last crash was intentional, all of them were." she asked? More forlorn this time, the devastation of this season is setting in. Ha! And she thought Dougie was going to be the worst of her problem this year, oh was she wrong.

Dougie shook his head yes, "He saw us in on the

couch, the night you heard the footsteps, and he assumed that if we were an item," he motioned between the two of them, "That I wouldn't go to the Langles with him."

Her heart broke into a million pieces. He would leave just like everyone else. She didn't want to be a pick me girl but damn for one moment in her life, Grace wanted to be picked. To not have any other choice but love. She wanted to kiss him in all the places she had imagined every night, curl up in his arms when she felt unsafe.

"I didn't know about any of this Grace, I swear on my life." He looked at her misty eyed and scared. "Me and you... it's the first real thing in my life besides racing." He reached out to take her hands again as if grabbing on to a lifeline. "I can't lose this; I'll do anything to prove to you I didn't know about his plans."

She hated to admit it, but she felt inclined to believe

him, and it would be a simple call in the morning over to the Langles to see how this all started anyways. Maybe she would save that phone call for next week. There was no rush at this point, they could certainly have Tanner. He was no longer welcome in any car of hers. But she knew in her gut what Dougie was saying was true.

Besides the initial attitude, he had done nothing for her not to trust him. He had given her a hard time, but he never failed to be open and honest with every question she had when it came to the races.

"But what about when you suggested to me that he threw the race?" She hadn't meant to ask out loud, but it was too late now.

Dougie shrugged, "he won the next one and then we got caught up in us. I never continued to investigate it or press him further about it." He was right. They had gotten caught up in themselves so much that they stopped looking into the losses. What a rookie mistake.

They should have spent more time looking into what was going on with Tanner and the car. They should have seen something coming, some sign. But getting lost in his caramel eyes brought Grace to her knees. This was the type of love grandmothers told stories about to their grandbabies, where hands fit perfectly together.

"I don't know what to do about next season," She laughed, sarcastically. As if they had any options available at all.

"I've already called us out of the last race of this season, Driftwood Bay will still host but we won't be racing. We have back up drivers believe it or not. Tanner scared them all away with his antics." She scoffed.

"We'll figure out a new driver together. Tanner can go race with the Langles, fuck them. STJRacing is my home and that's where I'm going to stay. I love you Princess, I guess I have for a long time, but I didn't know how to show it. Or say it." His eyes met hers.

Her heart melted. How could such a grumpy gruff say all the right things to make her heart sing.

"I love you too."

Stay tuned for Tanner's story coming
February 2024!

Driftwood Bay

Race To My Heart

Picking Up The Pieces – Winter 2024 (Tanners Story)

Printed in Great Britain
by Amazon

27264227R00117